Other books by ALBERT MALTZ

The Cross and the Arrow
The Journey of Simon McKeever
A Long Day in a Short Life
Man on a Road and Other Stories
A Tale of One January
The Underground Stream

The Eyewitness Report

A NOVEL

Albert Maltz

Introduction by Patrick Chura

CALDER PUBLICATIONS
an imprint of

ALMA BOOKS LTD
Thornton House
Thornton Road
Wimbledon Village
London SW19 4NG
United Kingdom
www.calderpublications.com

Represented by:
Authorised Rep Compliance Ltd
Ground Floor
71 Lower Baggot Street
Dublin, D02 P593
Ireland
www.arccompliance.com

The Eyewitness Report first published by Calder Publications in 2025

© The Estate of Albert Maltz, 2025
Introduction © Patrick Chura, 2025
Notes and map © Alma Books Ltd, 2025

Front cover: David Wardle

Printed in Great Britain by CPI Group (UK) Ltd, Croydon CR0 4YY

ISBN: 978-0-7145-5096-1

All rights reserved. No part of this publication may be reproduced, stored in or introduced into a retrieval system, or transmitted, in any form or by any means (electronic, mechanical, photocopying, recording or otherwise), without the prior written permission of the publisher. This book is sold subject to the condition that it shall not be resold, lent, hired out or otherwise circulated without the express prior consent of the publisher.

Contents

The Eyewitness Report

Introduction	VII
THE EYEWITNESS REPORT	I
Author's Note	5
Map of Red Square and the surrounding area	6
Chapter 1	7
Chapter 2	25
Chapter 3	41
Chapter 4	57
Chapter 5	69
Chapter 6	89
Chapter 7	103
Chapter 8	127
Chapter 9	147
Chapter 10	161
Notes	177

Introduction

The cultural-political movement known as the "Prague Spring" came into being on 5th January 1968, when reformist statesman Alexander Dubček was elected First Secretary of the Communist Party of Czechoslovakia. Dubček's liberalizations – freedom of speech, multi-party elections, an uncensored media and constraints on the dreaded secret police – amounted to an ambitious programme that promised to reinvigorate democratic socialism and offer citizens "a fuller life of the personality" than was possible in the capitalist West or in the increasingly illiberal Soviet Union.

Exactly seven months, two weeks and two days after its birth, Dubček's dream of "socialism with a human face" died a violent death, crushed by half a million Soviet-led Warsaw Pact troops. Dubček was arrested, one hundred and thirty-seven civilians were killed, and seventy thousand Czechoslovakians fled immediately to the West.

So ended a brave experiment. But as the *New York Times* predicted, the tyrannical crackdown was "certain to provoke an outcry not only from non-Communists, but also from Communists around the world".

In Moscow, the fledgling Human Rights Movement was energized. Since that April, Natalya Gorbanevskaya and a group of activists had been circulating carbon copies of the *Chronicle of Current Events*, an underground samizdat newsletter that exposed human-rights abuses by the Soviet government.

On the night of 21st August, while caring for her three-month-old son and listening to Soviet media reports of the "fraternal intervention" in Prague, Gorbanevskaya typed notes for the *Chronicle*, then fashioned a home-made Czech flag and mounted it on a stick. The next morning she made two more cloth banners, one of which read, "Long Live Free and Independent Czechoslovakia". The other carried her favourite slogan: "For Your Freedom and Ours".

On the 25th, a Sunday, Gorbanevskaya folded the flag and the banners, slipped them under the mattress of her baby carriage and wheeled the carriage towards Red Square. On the way she saw people she knew and smiled at them. Her little boy slept peacefully. She came to the appointed meeting place, the old "Execution Ground" monument, just as her friends Pavel Litvinov and Larisa Bogoraz and several others were approaching. The clock struck twelve. It took a few seconds to unfurl the banners. She gave hers to comrades and kept only the Czech flag for herself, holding it in one hand, with her other on the stroller. Then, in a single movement, the eight demonstrators sat down on the raised parapet encircling the monument and displayed their outrage: "Hands Off Czechoslovakia", "Down with the Occupiers".

Almost immediately, they heard shouts of anger and saw people racing towards them. The first to be assaulted was Viktor Fainberg, a literature student recently arrived from Leningrad, who was tackled and kicked in the head. Gorbanevskaya saw him on the ground as the banners were torn away and her flagstick broken. She would always remember the sound of ripping cloth.

* * *

Readers of *The Eyewitness Report* will learn what happened to Gorbanevskaya and her comrades after their banners were destroyed. The protagonist and titular "eyewitness" is forty-two-year-old Daniil Petrovich Barkov, a prizewinning Soviet writer whose life is at a crossroads. As the novel begins, his wife, Anna, is slowly dying in a hospital bed, and his faith in his country has been shaken by the shameful violation of Czech sovereignty four days earlier.

INTRODUCTION

Standing at the Execution Ground near St Basil's Cathedral, Barkov is approached by a sightseer and asked about the significance of the monument. It had been built in the sixteenth century, Barkov professorially explains, and "had served as a place of execution, but also had been used for the proclamation of edicts and the announcement of the call to arms".

Within the novel each of these historical purposes will metaphorically recur and resonate. Barkov witnesses, but does not join, a peaceful protest with violent consequences. He has been reading samizdat literature, but in order to protect Anna from anxiety, he has not become a member of the Human Rights Movement. Stirred by the bravery of the demonstrators, he shouts "Why beat them?" – a naive question that underscores his lack of genuine political commitment.

The first point of direct contact between Maltz's fictional character and factual history (there will be many) is when Barkov, sensing physical danger to one protester in particular, whispers urgently to the young mother, Gorbanevskaya: "Please, girl, go away. Why should you sit, if you don't have to?" Her clear and confident rejoinder, "A public demonstration is needed!" stuns Barkov and stokes his inner turmoil.

The second point of contact between Barkov and an actual demonstrator symbolizes his potential for growth. The most brutal moment in the 25th August protest was the beating of the only Jewish participant, Viktor Fainberg: "Was it five or a dozen times they kicked him," Barkov wonders, "before everyone heard the sickening crack as his upper front teeth snapped off at the gum line?"

On his way home, the celebrated Soviet author examines his conscience. He rationalizes that the net value of the protest did not equal the price the protesters would pay for it, but he can't shake off more difficult questions. Did he have the moral right to keep silent in the presence of political evil? Were his mental gymnastics no more than an effort to comfort himself, because he had not had their courage?

Barkov returns to the Execution Ground. There is something he must retrieve. Fearing detection, he furtively bends down and rescues from the bloody pavement "two of the jagged crimson teeth that had dropped from the mouth of the man with a hooked nose and a strong character". Instead of being the kind of writer whose works are taught in Soviet schools, he will now go the way of the dissident, with Fainberg's upper incisors as his talisman. He is unaware that he is already a target of the state.

* * *

The strangulation of the Prague Spring has inspired visual art, music, drama and prose, including the novels of Milan Kundera and the plays of Václav Havel. With the first-ever publication of *The Eyewitness Report*, Maltz joins Kundera and Havel among world-class artists moved by the Prague spirit.

In a journal Maltz kept while working on the novel, he committed himself to an art that would "keep faith" with political victims. He cited as inspirations Viktor Fainberg and Pavel Litvinov of Red Square, but also singled out Petro Grigorenko, the Red Army general who was locked away in a psychiatric hospital and stripped of his citizenship for telling the truth. He named anti-fascist literature professor Eduard Goldstücker, a leader of the Prague Spring, who was forced into exile when the Soviet tanks rumbled in. Andrei Sakharov and Mstislav Rostropovich, who endured harassment and exile after speaking out for Prague and for civil liberties, were likewise in Maltz's thoughts.

And in the case of Alexander Solzhenitsyn, whose persecution is a key background factor in *The Eyewitness Report*, Maltz had already demonstrated solidarity. In December 1972, Maltz learnt that the dissident novelist, expelled from the Soviet Writers' Union and denied his royalties, was cash-strapped and desperate. Identifying with Solzhenitsyn's plight as an author "suffering from blacklisting in its most acute form... in his own country", Maltz publicly offered to donate to Solzhenitsyn his uncollected Soviet royalties (about 34,000 roubles, the equivalent of around $37,750) to relieve the banned writer's hardships. The US media celebrated the gesture, but retaliation from the USSR was swift. All of Maltz's contracts with Moscow publishers were quickly cancelled.

In the context of *The Eyewitness Report*, this is important for several reasons. Maltz completed the novel in 1973 and was unusually excited about it. After two decades on the Cold War blacklist, he had finally found a commercial publisher for a collection of his short stories in 1970, but he believed this new novel would be his true return to relevance, if not prominence. In letters to friends, he solicited coaching for his planned appearances on the TV talk-show circuit when *The Eyewitness Report* hit the bookstores.

From late 1973 through 1975, at least a dozen American publishers rejected Maltz's novel. Some felt that, with Solzhenitsyn in vogue internationally, Maltz's manuscript was ill-timed: "The problems of current oppression and tyranny in the Soviet Union have been too recently treated," explained an editor at Bobbs-Merrill in 1974.

The real problem with *The Eyewitness Report* was the nationality of its author. One US publisher wrote, "I find it difficult to accept fully the idea of an American novelist assuming the guise of a Soviet writer." Maltz's London agent Robert Harben explained that editors were "reluctant… because the book has not been written by someone living in Russia". Though Harben dubbed this "a foolish argument", it was insurmountable. At Doubleday, the largest US publisher, a senior editor mused, "If only it had been written by one who had lived through it…"

Of course, Maltz *had* lived through it. As one of the Hollywood Ten, a group of film-industry figures who challenged the constitutional legitimacy of the US House Un-American Activities Committee in 1947, he was fined, jailed for ten months and thwarted as a writer for twenty years. His crime?

Refusing to cooperate with the congressional investigation into alleged communist subversion.

Like Daniil Barkov, winner of a Stalin Prize and a Lenin Prize, Maltz was a gifted artist – "a man whose talent has made a contribution to the cultural life of his country" – who was eventually shunned in his own nation of birth. And in Maltz's extraordinary case, he had just been blacklisted by the Soviet Union as well.

In *The Eyewitness Report*, Maltz registers with precision Barkov's frustration at being reduced to a non-person – because he has felt that frustration himself. The editors who rejected the novel on the basis of Maltz's American identity failed to see it as, in part, a work of autobiographical fiction about the soul of a banned artist.

As early as April 1969, Maltz claimed a connection with Soviet dissident writers, going on record at a public forum in support of Yuli Daniel and Andrei Sinyavsky, who were sentenced to hard labour for publishing works satirizing Soviet society. Here is how Maltz explained their persecution:

> I cannot avoid the observation that to a considerable extent they behaved as did the members of the Hollywood Ten when they were blacklisted by the film industry. They were prosecuted under a law prohibiting "agitation or propaganda" for purposes of "subversion" – does this or does it not sound like a hearing before the Committee on Un-American Activities? I cannot, out of my own personal history, fail to make common cause with these imprisoned Russian writers.

In the summer of 1973, Maltz sent the half-completed manuscript of *The Eyewitness Report* to Eduard Goldstücker, the former president of the Czech Writers' Union, and to a number of former Soviet citizens who were living in Moscow in 1968, asking whether the pages seemed "valid" to them and explaining: "I would not have undertaken this novel unless I felt that my own experiences, and the various sources of information available to me, would allow me to write it with verisimilitude to the Soviet scene, history and experience."

Maltz did not foresee the wall he would hit among parochial US publishers who apparently felt that only a Soviet citizen could write convincingly about political tyranny. He did anticipate what he called "the flak" that would come from doctrinaire leftists.

Long accustomed to being vilified by the political right, who would not forgive him for being a communist, Maltz would now have to explain himself to the radical left, who might well vilify him for being a *former* communist. Before he'd even finished the novel, he made ready: "I must be prepared for many good people who will consider my book harmful," he wrote in his journal, "as well as for the vituperation and slanders that will hit me from the socialist countries and from rigid communists everywhere."

In answer to expected charges that his novel was anti-communist, he rehearsed counter-arguments:

> Were *The Grapes of Wrath* and *Native Son* anti-American books? Why should we protest the US war in Vietnam, the murders at Kent State, the fascist takeover in Greece... and keep silent about the Soviet Union?
>
> I must unfurl in my book the banner of healthy human socialism and the credo of a freethinking socialist. I will be telling my readers that socialism does not have to be deformed... that it can be humanist.
>
> I will pay a terrible price for this book if I cannot take the criticism calmly, without tension. Criticism from tyrants or rigid communist believers will only confirm the soundness of my book and the morality of my position.
>
> However, my book cannot lend itself to the support of capitalism.

In the same set of notes, Maltz acknowledged that he came of age as an artist as a member of the American Communist Party, a political culture in which criticism of the Soviet Union was suppressed: "But if we had known that the Stalin trials were frame-ups and that millions of people were imprisoned, tortured, shot, under his tyrannical rule, would we have remained silent then? I wouldn't have!"

Clearly, Maltz understood that fascism was fascism, whether it came from Nazi Germany, the Soviet Union or the United States. He knew it when he saw it. In *The Eyewitness Report*, he called it out. Fifty years later, the novel is more relevant than ever.

– Patrick Chura, University of Akron

The Eyewitness Report[*]

> *Many mistakes have been made in the world which now one would hardly think a child could make. How many crooked, narrow, impassable blind alleys, leading far off the track, has mankind chosen in the effort to reach the eternal verity!...*
>
> NIKOLAI GOGOL[*]

*To
my wife, Esther**

Author's Note

This is a work of fiction, and therefore the characters and story have been invented. However, the facts involved are true, and there is ample documentation to support them. I am especially indebted to B.K.R.,* without whose personal experiences this novel could not have been written.

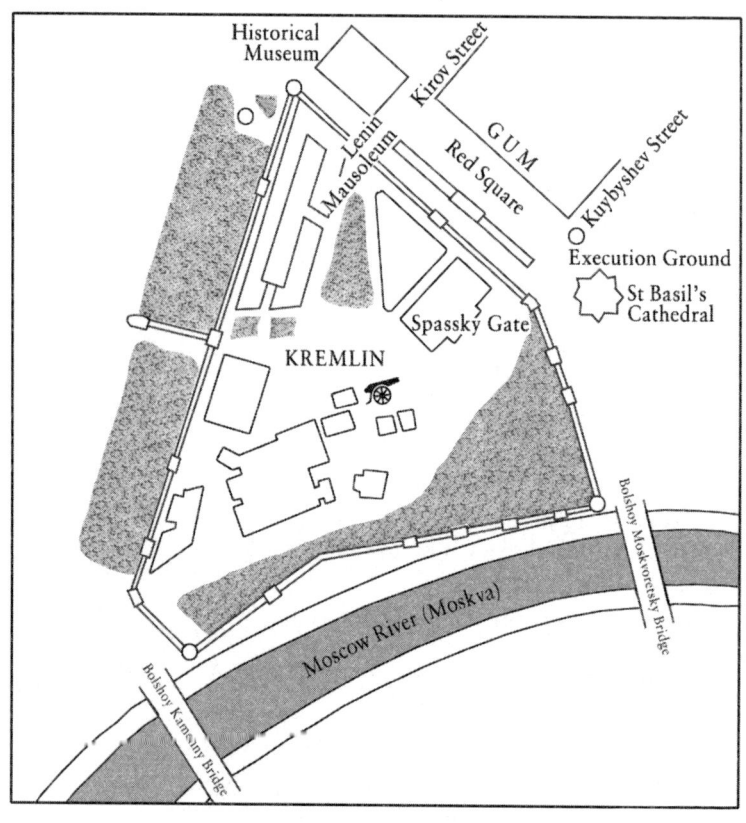

Map of Red Square and the surrounding area
(based on the map in Natalya Gorbanevskaya's
book *Red Square at Noon*, p. 44)

Chapter 1

I

*25th August 1968**

Barkov was excited and nervous. The note that had been dropped into his letter box the day before had been unsigned and printed in anonymous block letters. It said: "Noon tomorrow – Red Square." He had been astonished. Nothing like that ever had happened to him before. He had taken the note into the toilet at once, burnt it and flushed the ashes away.

Now it was eleven fifty, and he was standing on the top step of the ancient monument called "Execution Ground",* which provided the best view of the whole of Red Square. Everything looked normal. The day being Sunday, the GUM department store was closed, but the Lenin Mausoleum was open. For this reason, the right side of the immense rectangle before him, over four hundred yards long, had only a moderate number of strolling pedestrians, while the lower half of the other side had a close-packed queue of people six abreast that stretched from the Tomb to the Historical Museum and then curved out of sight into the gardens alongside the Kremlin wall. Thirty yards behind him was the exquisite cathedral of St Basil with the usual throng of visitors filing in or out or taking photographs. To his left, a hundred yards off, there was a heavy flow of tourists, both Russian and foreign, entering and leaving the grounds of the Kremlin itself through the Spassky Gate. Normal, altogether normal – pigeons being fed here and there, an elderly vendor of balloons sitting on a box. Aside from several militiamen directing the sparse auto traffic, there were no agents of AUTHORITY to be seen – no blue-uniformed members of the Committee of State Security, no obvious plain-clothes men, and certainly no armed soldiers except for the two white-gloved statues who were standing their hour of formal guard at the doorway to Lenin's Tomb. For this reason, he felt certain that there *would* be some sort of event when the hour struck.

Why had the unknown person dropped a note into his letter box instead of knocking on his door? He had been home most of the previous day and evening. It was true that the courier might have come during the hour he had gone to Gorky Street to send a cable. Possible, but not likely. It was a better guess that the individual was someone he did not know, and therefore would not have trusted. Or the opposite: someone wanted to get this information to him, but did not trust *him* enough. However, from these bits and pieces he could deduce a number of things. First, the secrecy meant that the event scheduled for noon would be one over which the State Security Police would take jurisdiction. Second, quite possibly it might be related to the shameful affair of four days before: the occupation of Czechoslovakia by Soviet troops and tanks. And third, those who had prepared the event had hoped for something from him.

What?

He didn't know, but intense curiosity had brought him here in spite of the nervous tension he felt. The tension was illogical, because any citizen could come to Red Square freely on a Sunday or any other day. Moreover, he was an author, and the anthology of poetry under his arm was a natural stage prop for a man of letters out for a stroll. Nevertheless, old apprehensions lingered in the recesses of his soul. Stalin's rule had been too cruel for too many years, even though it never had scarred him personally. To the contrary, the old man had been charmingly benign on the one occasion in which he had met him.

CHAPTER I

Still, why had the note been dropped into his box? In order to protect Anna from anxiety he had not become a member of the newly formed Human Rights Movement, nor had he joined others in the several years past in signing letters of protest against various repressive acts of the authorities. Was *that* the clue? Did they want someone on Red Square who was both well known to the public and was considered to be politically orthodox? If so, who were THEY, and what did THEY know about his private thinking – and from whom?

Barkov brushed a fly from his bare forearm and wiped his brow with the back of his hand. It was hot. The day before had been somewhat cloudy, and he had not anticipated the warmth of today's noonday sun. Bareheaded, he already was perspiring.

Like many Russians, Barkov was broad-shouldered, muscular, not very tall. His strongly carved face with its dimpled chin was unlined and youthful for his forty-two years and contrasted attractively with his prematurely grey hair. Despite several features he himself mildly disliked – irregular teeth, longish nose, brown eyes that he considered too small and deep-set – he was in fact a virile-looking, personable man.

Two hundred yards down the Square a taxi stopped close to the Lenin Mausoleum. It caught Barkov's attention and stimulated a fantasy. What if someone were to race up the stairs to the top of the tomb and shout some protest to the people below? Had it ever happened in the half-century of the Soviet Union?

The door of the taxi opened, and a young man in a dark suit stepped out. After him came a girl, hair bleached platinum, wearing a white bridal gown, with a bouquet of flowers in her hand. The couple walked side by side up to the militiaman who was supervising the two lines of people entering and leaving the tomb. The traffic officer turned to them, listened for a moment, then waved his white glove. The bride walked a little to the side, knelt and placed her flowers in front of the red granite wall of the Mausoleum. Then the couple walked back to the taxi and drove off – to a happy, conjugal future, Barkov hoped. He found the gesture moving. On their wedding day, a bride and groom express their dedication to socialism and their reverence for its great leader. Why not? At the same time, he was irritated by the adulation of icons that was inherent in the act. More than once he had composed a letter to *Pravda** pointing out that this enshrinement of a Communist in place of St George* left intact a centuries-old humility before AUTHORITY. Lenin himself would have abhorred this Byzantine use of his mummified corpse. It was a good letter, but naturally he had composed it in his mind, not on paper, and never had sent it.

It was still six minutes before noon. A young soldier on leave strolled past Execution Ground hand in hand with a bright-eyed, pretty girl of seventeen. At once Barkov remembered the bleak whiteness of the snowy day, twenty-seven years before, when he had seen his wife for the first time. He had paused, pick in hand, and gazed down into the anti-tank trench, where she was shovelling the frozen earth with such concentration and effort. His heart had given a great thump, and he had thought, "What an angel!" She was dying now, his cherished Anna, and there was no way that medical science could reverse the downward slide. He would, with love, visit her daily in the hospital until the present crisis was over, and he could take her home; he would hold her hands and kiss them with a lump in his throat; he would report conversations, read poetry, make her smile – and yet each night, not without guilt, he would hold another woman close. Side by side in his heart were anguish over his wife and happiness over a new-found and desperately needed love – and he would not attempt to deny the intensity of either emotion. If this was not the nature of all men, it was his.

A group of some twenty people was approaching him from the direction of the Mausoleum. After an appraising glance, he guessed that they were from a collective farm and were in Moscow for an outing.

"Pardon me, comrade..."

CHAPTER I

The farm group had paused at the steps. A brawny man of fifty with a mouthful of steel teeth was smiling up at him. "What are you standing on?"

"Execution Ground."

"What's that?"

Barkov, who had a quiet, almost professorial manner of speaking, explained that the circular structure had been built in the sixteenth century, had served as a place of execution, but also had been used for the proclamation of edicts and the announcement of the call to arms.

Several of the adolescent boys raced up the half-dozen steps, where a closed gate prevented access to the flat stone top. Barkov smiled at the disappointment on their faces. Obviously they had hoped to see something dramatic. He gestured towards the Spassky Gate. "Look over there, boys, at those soldiers. You don't want to miss that, it's the changing of the guard in front of Lenin's Tomb."

The boys hurtled down the steps with a shout. Everyone else in the group followed with instant excitement, the brawny man gesturing his appreciation.

The squad of three smartly tailored, white-gloved soldiers that had sauntered out of the Spassky Gate came to a halt. Their uniforms were greenish-blue, like those of the two guards at Lenin's Tomb, and were ornamented with gold belts and gold braid. The officer checked his watch, then stiffened and raised his rifle to his left shoulder. Immediately the two soldiers behind him did the same. The officer raised his right arm across his chest and grasped the gun. The two soldiers did likewise. Instantly, as though a fuse had been ignited in all of them at once, they launched into a high, resounding goose-step as they marched with absolute precision towards the Mausoleum a hundred yards off. Barkov turned his eyes away. He detested that wretched style of parading. Under the tsars, high-ranking officers had studied at German military academies – hence the adoption of the goose-step. Yet, whenever he saw it, he wondered by what quirk the Kremlin leaders could continue to use this symbol of Prussian militarism after the horrors of World War Two. Tradition become idiocy!

It was three minutes before noon. He noticed a woman with a baby carriage coming towards him from the direction of GUM. She was moving quickly. Almost immediately he saw some men and one woman rapidly approaching Execution Ground from the centre of the Square. He looked behind. No one was coming from there. He glanced towards the Spassky Gate – no one. When the group in front was fifteen yards away, he noticed a face and knew at once that some sort of activity was going to take place directly in front of him. The man he recognized had been pointed out to him in a theatre lobby – Pavel Litvinov,* a young physicist, grandson of the most celebrated of Soviet diplomats. Barkov was astonished to see him there. It was common knowledge that Litvinov had been dismissed from an important academic post because he was a self-proclaimed active member of the Human Rights Movement. The dismissal had been a punishment for his aggressive criticism of the court proceedings in a political case. Since he had no job, he was open to the penal charge of being a social parasite, and could be sentenced to five years' exile in Siberia – or, if the judge was vindictive, to a similar term in prison. Yet, instead of hiding his face from AUTHORITY, here he was on Red Square.

Barkov ran down the stairs. The people below had moved in so close to the curving wall of Execution Ground that he had lost sight of some of them. He was surprised to see that the woman with the baby carriage was now in the centre of the group. As she lifted an infant out of the carriage, the others quickly raised the pallet inside and took out a number of small cloth banners. The pallet was put back in place, and the sleeping baby laid down again. Then, as the bells in the tower of the Spassky Gate began to chime the noon hour, the eight men and women in front of Barkov positioned themselves side by side with their backs to Execution Ground. In silence they

CHAPTER I

sat down on the pavement and unfurled banners protesting the occupation of Czechoslovakia.

Barkov stepped back a few yards, so that he would not block the view of anyone else. His throat felt choked at this reckless bravery. It could mean a prison term! A demonstration like this against a decision of the Kremlin was unprecedented. They might sit in a Siberian labour camp three years, five years – maybe more.

The young, round-faced mother,* short in stature, wearing large eyeglasses on her plain peasant's face, sat next to the carriage. She held a small Czech flag in her hand. There were only three banners among the seven other demonstrators – home-made affairs of white calico fastened at each end to sticks. Litvinov, a husky, good-looking man, was in the centre of the curving line. He held a banner that said "For Your Freedom and Ours". Beside him was a smiling woman whose slogan read "Hands Off Czechoslovakia". Barkov felt he had seen her before also. She appeared to be the oldest of the group, about forty,* her body chubby, her greying black hair a bit unkempt. The last banner was held by a young, slender man* at the far end of the curving line. It read "Down with the Occupiers". Alongside him was an attractive girl who looked like a student,* and beside her a tall man in his late twenties.* Further on there were two more men, both approaching forty,* one very nearsighted, dark-haired, and with a hooked nose so that he might have been an Armenian or a Georgian, a Jew or an Arab. The last one was largely bald, with a steady grin that conveyed defiance.

Some spectators already had gathered, half a dozen or so, and more were coming. It became clear to Barkov why the eight had chosen this spot for their demonstration. Execution Ground was surrounded by a five-foot width of raised pavement that made it a natural traffic island. Therefore they might be successfully defended against a charge that they had disrupted vehicular traffic on the Square. It also was likely that

13

the symbolism of their protest had not been lost upon them. Where better to express their indignation over the execution of another nation's freedom than in front of a tsarist monument where executions had been carried out in public?

The last chimes of noon were drifting away. Instantly, shrill police whistles were heard from various parts of the Square. Barkov turned to look. Several men in civilian clothes were racing towards them at full speed from the direction of the Mausoleum. Others, with a burly woman behind them, were running from the direction of GUM.

What happened from then on was, for Barkov, like watching a motion picture in which furious physical action was photographed by a hand-held, swiftly moving camera, so that some things were lost in a blur of motion while others were indelibly printed on his mind's eye, and in which the words spoken were sometimes crystal-clear and sometimes bedlam.

The unseen whistles were still blowing when the first of the hard-running civilians reached the scene. All were athletic men under thirty, neatly dressed in summer sport clothes. With one accord they began to shout loudly as they ripped the banners from the seated demonstrators.

"Anti-Soviet hooligans – you've sold yourselves for dollars!"

"You dog shit, how dare you come to Red Square where foreign tourists can see you?"

And directly to the spectators: "They're all Yids. What they need is an honest Russian fist in their ugly snouts."

With fury they tore the banners to shreds and hurled them to the pavement. Barkov, with his teeth clenched, watched the thugs – whom everyone knew to be State Security Police in plain clothes – while the derisive epithet "Yids" echoed in his inner ear. Was this the year 1908? Were these the tsar's organized hoodlums... the Black Hundreds* his father had told him about... the scum Lenin had denounced?

By this time the second group had arrived, and both together began beating the demonstrators in a vicious yet random fashion, as though it was a matter of personal impulse. The women, and several of the men, were not touched. But the bald-headed man was kicked so hard in the abdomen that a low cry came from the lips that until then had been smiling. Litvinov was struck in the face alternately by two of the Security policemen – a man using his briefcase as a weapon and the brawny, snub-nosed woman swinging her large handbag. (Barkov wondered with a sick heart whether the ghost of Litvinov's grandfather was watching from the top of Lenin's Tomb.) The slender young man was kicked in the side and punched hard in the face.

"Why beat them?" Barkov shouted indignantly. "Why beat them?" His question was echoed hysterically by a woman behind him, but the KGB agents did not reply. Instead, two of them leapt at the nearsighted man with the hooked nose.

"Look at him! A Zionist provocateur on Red Square! There isn't any insult they aren't up to."

Neither used his hands on the man, but like a practised team one kicked him repeatedly in the body and the other in the face. Seated, with his back to the wall of Execution Ground, he automatically raised his hands in ineffective defence, but did nothing else.

Was it five or a dozen times they kicked him – Barkov didn't know – before everyone heard the sickening crack as his upper front teeth snapped off at the gum line? Blood poured from his mouth, spattering the blouse of the woman beside him and falling on his trousers and the pavement.

"My God, what are you doing?" a woman in the crowd screamed as she burst into sobs.

Abruptly the violence stopped. "Autos, commandeer some autos," a pleasant-looking KGB man said calmly. Four of the ten ran off at full speed in the direction of GUM, where there always was some traffic going to or coming from Kuybyshev Street.

Dazed, yet with a peculiar little smile on his swollen, blood-smeared lips, the nearsighted man groped for the four crimson teeth lying scattered on the stone between his knees. Watching him, Barkov wondered if he had the talent to write a Dostoevskian novel about a group of Security agents like these men. Some had started out as idealists, no doubt, and still considered themselves defenders of the socialist state against its enemies.

The number of spectators had increased to about thirty, with some asking, "What's going on here?"

"They're Czechs," Barkov heard. "We lost two hundred thousand dead liberating them from the Nazis, but now they want to make a counter-revolution. They're in the pay of the CIA."

"So off with them to prison," a voice nearby demanded loudly. It belonged to a young six-footer with the wind-burnt skin of one who works out of doors. He popped a sunflower seed into his mouth and cracked it expertly with his strong teeth.

Now a dialogue began that sometimes brought an exchange between individuals, but at other times was like the chanting of three choral groups paying no attention to one another. The Security Police, partially turning their backs on the demonstrators, began to harangue the crowd in an obvious attempt not only to convince them that the protesters were enemies of the Soviet state, but also to incite a physical attack on them. Most of the spectators were silent, but some among them talked to the police, to the demonstrators, or to one another. As for the demonstrators, they spoke in quiet tones, trying to explain to the spectators why they were there, what they were doing.

"What are you sitting there for?" a plump, pretty woman called out. There were tears on her cheeks. "Explain yourselves, comrades." It was obvious to Barkov that she had some tie to the group.

"Am I hearing right?" one of the KGB agents shouted indignantly. "You call them comrades? Be ashamed! They're tools of the Czech and German fascists."

"We're holding a peaceful demonstration, but our banners have been taken away by violence," said the chubby woman with greying hair. She continued to talk as several of the Security Police tried with considerable success to drown her out. "Our papers and radios report that there is unanimous support for sending our troops into Czechoslovakia. But it *isn't* unanimous! That's why we are here. We're honest Soviet citizens – we're not tools of anyone."

"Ha, listen to that parasite," the snub-nose with the handbag shouted. "Look how brazen she is as she slanders our government. She should be sent to cut trees in Siberia!"

The voice of the pleasant-looking man, who seemed to be in command, boomed out: "They're anti-Soviets, they ought to be smashed."

The man who had been kicked in the stomach raised his voice. "Listen, citizens, the entry of Soviet troops into Czechoslovakia violates the right of nations to self-determination."

"Lice! Anti-Soviet lice!" the tall, young man alongside Barkov shouted with indignation. "My father lost an eye liberating Prague, and now you spit on his suffering. I know about you stuck-up intelligentsia." He gestured towards the Kremlin. "That's where the real brains are! What right have you got to oppose your pinhead ideas to theirs?" He shook both fists at them. "If *they* say the Czechs are selling out to German capitalism, that's enough for me. Instead of supporting the leaders who gave you your free education, you betray them!"

"Read the Constitution," Litvinov told him quietly. "Article 125 guarantees all citizens freedom of demonstration."

"I know the freedom you mean," the man with the briefcase snapped. "The freedom to slander, to create disturbances!" He kicked Litvinov in the leg.

Snub-Nose began addressing the crowd, which now numbered about fifty persons. "If these people are honest, why aren't they sitting down in front of the American Embassy to protest the murder of the Vietnamese?* Our boys are being received with flowers by the grateful Czech people!"

"Are they?" asked the young mother. "Then why did *Izvestia** report two days ago that the Czechs have been chalking swastikas on our tanks and refusing drinking water to our soldiers?"

The man beside Barkov cracked a sunflower seed and yelled angrily, "There isn't one of you intelligentsia I would trust – there isn't one of you who's sweated for his bread. I hope they give you twenty years and you die out there!"

"They're cockroaches – they should be stamped out!" said the agent in charge.

There was, however, no stir of activity in the small crowd. Most of the people had bland faces and seemed basically unconcerned, merely watching with curiosity as any crowd watches the unusual. And if some were privately unsettled at the sight of blood, it was not enough for them to challenge the Security Police.

At this moment Barkov caught sight of his near-neighbour, Sandler, at the rear of the crowd. As their eyes met, he knew at once who had dropped the note into his mailbox. Sandler was a research assistant in chemistry studying at Moscow university under a close friend of Barkov's. The latter, Ilya Krasny, had confided that he was collecting funds for the work of the newly formed Human Rights Movement. After Barkov had given him a substantial contribution, Krasny had asked if he was interested in receiving any of the self-published manuscripts the Movement was beginning to circulate. It was not illegal to distribute or to receive these uncensored documents, and Barkov was keenly interested in reading them. As a result, Sandler – a tall, shy Latvian – had been bringing him typewritten manuscripts from time to time. Since Barkov had been heavily preoccupied with Anna and his own work, he never had asked the young man in for a chat or a cup of tea. Yet it seemed obvious to him now that the demonstration had been hastily prepared, and that word about it had not travelled far. It must have been Sandler himself who personally decided to inform him about it – possibly with the hope that he would

CHAPTER I

write something for hand-to-hand circulation. That was, after all, the way important news got around these days.

A blue Volga driven by a middle-aged civilian stopped ten yards from Execution Ground. Two of the KGB agents who had raced off towards GUM jumped out and ran up to the man in charge. There was a whispered exchange, and the two gestured to some of their colleagues. Rapidly and roughly, they began to haul various of the unresisting demonstrators to their feet and rush them towards the waiting auto. The slender young man at the end of the line shouted to the crowd, "Our protest upholds the honour of our country. Down with aggression!" In reward for this sentiment, one of his arms was twisted behind his back until he cried out. Three more cars arrived, one of them bearing a traffic militiaman, who stood quietly and gazed at the crowd with an impassive face. All of the male demonstrators were struck repeatedly on the sides or back by the Security Police as they were hustled into the autos. When the man with the bleeding mouth was pulled to his feet, Barkov heard the pretty student ask in a trembling voice if he was badly hurt. She addressed him as Vitya,* which meant that she knew him well enough to use his nickname. His reply was too muffled to be heard. At the last moment Barkov suddenly recalled who the chubby woman of forty years was – Larisa Danielova, wife of the writer Yuli Daniel, who was in a prison camp. She had been pointed out to him the previous December on Constitution Day at Pushkin Square. So now she too was likely to sit!

The doors slammed, the autos turned around and moved off rapidly towards Kuybyshev Street. Only one car and three of the actors in the small drama still remained: the young mother – who, for some reason, had not been arrested – and two of the KGB: Snub-Nose and the man in charge. These two now began to pick up the scraps of cloth that a few minutes before had been brave banners.

Quickly Barkov moved over close to the mother. "Go away," he told her softly.

She gazed at him solemnly through her large eyeglasses and shook her head.

"Please, girl, go away," he whispered urgently. "Why should you sit, if you don't have to?"

"A public demonstration is needed!" she replied firmly. (Was she as calm as she appeared?) "The Czechs must know that some Russians at least have a conscience."

"They'll learn it through news of the others. One more arrested won't add anything."

The young woman shook her head, and Barkov stepped back into the crowd. He felt angry at her for her needless sacrifice, but he also felt tremendous admiration.

By this time the shreds of cloth had been gathered up. "So you're still here, you hooligan!" the man in charge said with annoyance. It seemed apparent that he would have preferred not to arrest a woman with an infant.

"Naturally she's still here!" It was Snub-Nose, speaking in a loud voice. "She came to exhibit herself – she's a slut."

The mother flushed. "How contemptible you are!"

"All right, stand up and get moving," the man told her irritably. "You're under arrest." Snub-Nose grabbed her arm and pulled her to her feet.

"I'm not leaving my baby," the mother shouted. "I have no one to leave him with, and I'm nursing him."

"How touching!" said Snub-Nose, letting go of her. "By all means, bring the little bastard and the carriage also. We'll take fine care of you."

Flanked by the two of them, the mother, head high, pushed her carriage to the waiting automobile. It was a blue Volga with white-curtained rear windows, indicating that it belonged to some official. The driver, a middle-aged man standing by the front door, was wearing the Medal of Valour on his dark, shabby jacket. He gazed at the mother with a fixed little smirk. Nevertheless, he opened the rear door for her. The mother picked up her infant and got inside. The carriage was folded

CHAPTER I

and lifted in after her. As the driver got behind the wheel and the two others went around to enter from the other side, the mother rolled down the rear window. In ringing tones she called out to the crowd, "Think about it, comrades! If the Czechs had been allowed to organize a democratic socialism, there'd be no excuse for the lack of freedom in our country. If—" The big hand of Snub-Nose struck her across the mouth and knocked off her eyeglasses. The window was rolled up, and the car started away.

2

The Kremlin chimes were sounding twelve fifteen. Barkov was standing in front of St Basil's Cathedral. After the mother's car had left, the militiaman had begun asking everyone to disperse. They had done so quietly. Barkov had wanted to speak to Sandler, but, when he turned around, the latter was twenty yards away, walking so rapidly that he decided not to follow. He expected to see him a few days from now anyway, when the third number of the *Chronicle of Current Events** came off the typewriters and began to circulate hand to hand. Sandler would come knocking at his door... and he would ask him about the other demonstrators. Of more importance to him at the moment was the desire to remain close to Execution Ground until another five or ten minutes had passed. He would then be able – without calling attention to himself – to stroll past the spot where the demonstrators had been sitting. He wanted to see something there.

Barkov felt wretched – sad, depressed, enraged, all at once. Despite his admiration for the moral fibre of the eight men and women, he felt that the net value of their protest simply did not equal the price they might have to pay. He was reminded of a simple observation that Anna had translated from the English and pasted on his desk many years before. It was by the American writer Thoreau: "The cost of a thing is the amount of life that is required to be exchanged for it."* What did the demonstration actually amount to beyond a quixotic gesture of self-expression? For their five minutes before fifty people, they probably would suffer one of two things: some years of harsh exile in Siberia or – worse – the bed of nails of a prison labour camp. If that happened, they would be isolated from others they could have influenced. Moreover, their entire lives would then be severely changed: the right to work at their professions, their freedom from constant surveillance by the Security Police, the ability to secure a liveable apartment or to travel outside the area of their immediate residence – everything. And to what purpose? How much more effective it would have been to agitate behind closed doors by means of hand-to-hand written materials.

Or was all of this no more than an effort to comfort himself because he had not had their courage? He could not deny that during one long, troubled moment when the mother had gazed at him so calmly and said "The Czechs must know that some Russians have a conscience", he had had a powerful impulse to sit down beside her and call out to the crowd, "I am Daniil Petrovich Barkov, and I, also, protest with indignation the use of our troops to strangle democracy in another socialist country." It would have caused a sensation. They could put the grandson of Litvinov on trial without ripples moving out to the far reaches of the land, but not an author whose *Letters to a Foreign Journalist** were required reading for every schoolchild – an author who had won a Stalin Prize and a Lenin Prize, and who had been immensely popular and widely read for twenty years!

Was it, then, a simple lack of courage? Had fatty tissue grown around his heart from too much success and good living?

He wouldn't presume to say it had not, but neither could he let himself be seduced by a sentimental pathos that defied the iron realities of life in Russia. What the demonstrators had done *was* quixotic, and he had been right not to join them.

CHAPTER I

How much more valuable it would be now to write a burning polemic and start circulating it! A way had been found at last to circumvent the damn censorship: self-publishing and hand-to-hand circulation were the new life-giving ingredients of Soviet intellectual life. With his name on a manuscript, so many copies would be made that it would be in every city of the country within a month – it would reach thousands of thinking people.

Barkov paused with a frown and rubbed his nose. For a heady moment he had forgotten Anna. Tension and anxiety were poison for her. It was for this reason they lived most of the year away from Moscow in the tranquillity of their Peredelkino* home. Yet now, when she was only two weeks out of a hepatic coma, and when he knew that she would remain an invalid until her death, he was churning with ideas that surely would hurtle him, and therefore her, into stormy waters. It was absurd. He could make no such decision without her consent.

But how depressing and disgusting it was that fifty-one years after a glorious revolution to achieve human brotherhood – a revolution, after all, that had given so much to the Soviet people – it seemed necessary to AUTHORITY to come running on the double to break up a peaceful demonstration of five men and three women. Actually, it was ludicrous – the all-powerful men in the Kremlin behaved as though any small whisper of dissent, if not smothered, would cause a revolutionary upheaval against them. The sad fact behind this was something he had discussed often with Anna and a few trusted friends – that the Party leaders knew only one way to rule: by command, without criticism or challenge from below. It was the only way they felt secure. And it had gone on like this for so many years that now they were afraid to change. Change itself seemed to them such a Pandora's box that they had not even been able to allow a test of democratic methods in another socialist country.

He looked at his watch: 12.23. He started to saunter back towards Execution Ground. Since he was carrying a book, he opened it, slowed his pace and pretended to be reading. There was no one around Execution Ground. Still pretending to read, he searched the pavement: the bloodstains had not yet congealed, and flies were taking nourishment from them. He saw what he was after: two of the jagged crimson teeth that had dropped from the mouth of a man with a hooked nose and strong character. Why had he come back for them – what did they mean to him? He couldn't put it into words. He could only say with Pascal: "The heart has its reasons, which reason knows nothing about."* He gazed around casually and knelt to adjust his shoelace. He picked up one tooth, then the second. Still reading, he strolled away.

Chapter 2

I

Barkov decided to walk along the river embankment for a while before going to the hospital to see his wife. He had an urgent need to resolve a conflict that had wedged deeper and deeper into his heart in the past several years, and now, suddenly, was too painful to ignore.

Next to his grief over his wife's illness, the most profound frustration in his life was the fact that he had yearned to be an author of the first rank and knew he was not. As a beginning writer he had dreamt of being compared one day to a Chekhov or a Tolstoy.* Yet, at his very best, he had reached the level, perhaps, of a Jack London.* Like London's fiction, his was dramatic, eminently readable, very popular — but it was too limited in scope, too lacking in psychological complexity and philosophic observation, to be of the first rank. This had not troubled him when he published his first volume of short stories, which was based upon his experiences as a front-line soldier in World War Two. He was still a student at Moscow University at the time, and to be published at all was sheer delight.

But as the years went on and he had several novels and other volumes of stories published, he began to realize that he was not growing as a writer. His work was well received by critics and always was popular with readers, but he was in a rut. In an effort to break out, he turned to the theatre. He wrote two historical dramas. In spite of his name, he could find no theatre willing to present the first one. The second was accepted, but was so severely hacked to pieces by the censors that he withdrew it in disgust before rehearsals began. Drifting, he spent the next several years writing children's novels. It was the one field of literature that gave authors more freedom than any other from the blue pencils of the Party watchdogs who decided what people could read. His books were printed in large editions, his savings account became fatter, but his disappointment in himself became keener. Since this type of writing did not require long hours at his desk, a good deal of his time went to self-indulgence – to conversation with Anna and a few friends, always with a bottle of cognac near his hand – and to one type of sport or another. He was a natural athlete, and he moved with the seasons from cross-country skiing to tennis and swimming. But he was deeply restless.

Without warning, everything changed. It was now three years since the concept of a large, complex, panoramic novel had set him on fire. He felt like a composer approaching his first symphony – suddenly, he could hear contrapuntal themes and swelling crescendos that he never had written before. The only way he could explain the change within himself was by the classic Marxist illustration of a pot of water slowly heating on a stove. When it finally came to a boiling point, the water turned to steam.

The novel, partly autobiographical, had the tentative title of *The Foundryman*. It was to be a portrait in depth of his father, and his father's multi-charactered world, from his birth in 1880 until his death in 1941. Barkov had done a year and a half of preparatory historical research, but, along with it, as a test of his ability to handle the materials, he had written four chapters set in different time periods. To his delight he found himself forging a new style. It provided a depth, and contained a probing of people and life, that had not been present in his previous work. Anna, Ilya Krasny and several other friends whose honesty he could trust agreed without reservation that he had made a remarkable leap forward.

CHAPTER 2

Yet, throughout those three years, he had been forced to cope with an increasing sense of guilt because of his failure as a man to measure up to the needs of his time. In the year 1965 two writers had been arrested, because it was discovered that they had published books under pseudonyms in the West* – books that were critical and satiric about life in the Soviet Union. In response to the arrests, a courageous scattering of individuals in Moscow, Leningrad and other centres came to the defence of the writers with public statements. Their numbers were small, but since they largely were of the intellectual elite, many of them scientists, they were important. Nevertheless, the two writers were convicted of subversion and slander and were sentenced to severe prison terms.

It was the beginning of a guerrilla warfare that still was going on. In all areas of intellectual life, the so-called "thaw" – which had existed under the anti-Stalinist leadership of Khrushchev* – began to be frosted over by a step-by-step return to authoritarianism. The "Signers" continued to oppose it. They were not an organized group – their name was derived merely from their public acts. Under Stalin they would have been shot. The current leadership was much less harsh, but repressive, nevertheless, in varied ways. Barkov's credo and conscience had made him want to be a Signer from the beginning. But that confronted him with an acute problem. If he became one, the novel he was writing might be rejected by all publishers by order of the Kremlin. If that happened, he could circulate it in manuscript form the way Solzhenitsyn* did with his unpublished novels. But Solzhenitsyn did not do this by choice, and he didn't want to either. It meant the difference between a limited, covert readership and an immense one. He desperately wanted this new, big work of his to be reviewed by critics, to be discussed at the Writers' Union, to be in all of the factory and farm libraries. For this reason he had accepted a way out of his dilemma that was provided by Anna's illness. Her physician had emphasized that anxiety and tension would harm her. It was a perfect excuse for him to lean upon – but he had been paying a penalty for it. Those who maintained silence inevitably supported the repressive actions of the authorities. He had been losing his self-esteem. He had appeased his guilt in part by his secret financial contribution to the Human Rights Committee. But only in part.

In the past four days, however, the uneasy equilibrium he had been maintaining had been shattered by a series of lightning bolts. On Wednesday he had awakened to the news of the brutal military occupation of Czechoslovakia. A second bolt had struck him only the day before – a letter from his dearest friend, Shika Botwin, a Pole living in Warsaw, with a tale of mistreatment that was horrifying. And now today he had witnessed behaviour on the part of the Security Police that could only be described as fascist.

The equilibrium was gone. If he was to keep his self-respect, he now had to join the ranks of the Signers. Anna knew about the occupation of Czechoslovakia. Like him she had been shocked by it. It surely would do her no harm to hear what he had witnessed on Red Square. Depending upon her reaction, he might be able to bring up the question of his writing an indictment of it.

2

There were many other strollers on the river embankment. Barkov wondered if any of them were troubled by the fact that there were Soviet tanks in Prague. Damned few, he was sure. He loved his fellow Russians, and was proud to have been born one of them, yet no people ever had lived who could not be led by the nose under certain conditions. AUTHORITY was insisting in an intensive propaganda campaign that reactionary Czechs, in league with West German fascists, had been preparing an anti-socialist coup. Buried under this massive lie was the simple truth that the majority of the Czech people,

CHAPTER 2

led by its own Communist Party, had begun to enjoy a socialism that was democratic. The lie had triumphed all too easily. What Russian didn't know that fascism was bestial? All aid to our Czech brothers then!

Meanwhile, it was delightful to saunter on the embankment, to watch a streamlined passenger launch cut a furrow in the sparkling water, to laugh and flirt if you were young or to sit on a park bench absorbed in a chessboard like the two men he was passing. Since the two looked to be over sixty, they would be receiving a state pension. One, he noted, must have been outstanding in his work, because he wore the medal of a Hero of Labour. If their wives were fifty-five, they also would be getting pensions. A couple could live quite well on such a joint stipend, but if they were factory workers and chose to continue on their jobs, they would receive full wages as well as their pensions. Was there any country in the West that cared for its elderly with such solicitude? There was a morality behind this that was not to be brushed aside by anyone – it had to be weighed.

Ah, but in his trouser pocket, wrapped now in a blue handkerchief, were two front teeth of a man named Viktor. And that, too, was an aspect of Soviet solicitude.

Barkov frowned and stopped walking. What if he had been under observation when he picked up the teeth – what if he were being followed now? He leant against the embankment wall. Shading his eyes with his hand, he turned half around and made a pretence of gazing at some buildings under construction. He could spot no face from Red Square and no one behind him had paused. He continued walking.

A boy on a bicycle slipped around him with so little space between them that he shouted with irritation "Watch what you're doing!" The youngster glanced back with a mischievous grin and shot away with reckless speed despite the number of pedestrians on the embankment.

That was a second item of bookkeeping – the fact that there were fewer children to be seen than was normal for a Sunday.

In how many capitalist countries did every urban child have a month's free vacation in the countryside? A few days from now the August campers would be pouring in at bus and train stations with their songs and banners. They would be sunburnt, well nourished, strong, ready to begin the school year. Had anything like that ever been witnessed under the tsars?

No, but something else had: the evil shout "They're all Yids!" Why hadn't that died when the tsars did? It was alien to Marxism, despised by Lenin, but, like a pustule under the skin, it grew or shrivelled according to the temperature of the times. In this summer of '68, it came all too smoothly from the tongue of a KGB agent on Red Square.

There was so much to love about his country that it split a man in half to hate what so needed to be hated.

To be torn in half was not comfortable. It created the automatic temptation to stop thinking, to renounce one's conscience and intellect in favour of AUTHORITY, and to comfort oneself by repeating that tomorrow surely would be better. But would it? What were the guarantees?

3

At the age of ten Barkov would have said that he had been born happy. No matter that in 1926 his mother had given birth to him in one of the clapboard-and-log houses of old Moscow with only a midwife in attendance. He was the child of strong, warm-hearted parents who loved him and loved their country, and knew with certainty that they were shaping both a good future for their son and a new society for mankind. The centuries-old dream of the pure in heart – equality and universal brotherhood – was being realized on Russian soil.

By the time he was five, Barkov knew that his father was a Communist Party member with the special title of "Old Bolshevik", and that he was the director of the huge foundry he was taken to see: glowing furnaces, molten metal being

CHAPTER 2

poured by big men into huge moulds – marvellously exciting! And when he was eight, in school and able to read ("Twenty years sooner than me," his father would say with pride, "not like under the tsars"), there was a tremendous event: they moved from their wooden house to a new apartment, where they had electric light and central heating and shared bathroom and kitchen with only one other family.

It was, for Barkov, the best of all circumstances in the best of all times, and he knew from his parents, as well as from his teachers, that it was due to the Communist Party and its great leader, the "man of steel".* Twenty-one years were to pass before he would change his mind. During those years fierce winds blew over the land. Enemies of the revolution, spies, foreign agents, were discovered on all sides and in the highest places. There was no Russian who did not know of this one or that arrested, including friends and relatives, a cousin of Barkov's father, two uncles on his mother's side, the director and vice-director of the whole metallurgical plant. It was disturbing and frightening, but faith in the Party made everyone conclude that those who were arrested, or who simply disappeared, had indeed been enemies of socialism. The day came, however, when every soul in Russia was shaken by a moral earthquake. It was revealed that the dead Stalin had been not only a man of steel, but a paranoid tyrant of terrifying ambition and cruelty, and that the phobias of this socialist dictator had travelled like an infection throughout the Party, so that millions of honest citizens had been sent to prison labour camps and untold numbers had been executed. Because he *was* a man of steel, dedicated in his own way to the humanist ideals of socialism, and because he had at his command a people capable of great deeds, the tyrant had helped transform Russia into a nation of such industrial strength that it triumphed in the most ferocious war in history. Yet, because of his cruelty and his manias, he had deformed socialism itself, and all of its leaders, in the process.

From that day on, Barkov knew that he had not been born to the best of all circumstances, and he swore to himself that for the rest of his life he never again would accept the politics of the Kremlin on faith. He might be forced to remain silent, but he would not allow himself to be duped.

4

He paused at an ice-cream cart on the embankment and queued up, about the twelfth in line. He heard chuckles and laughter and followed the gaze of the others. Five yards to the side of the cart, a drunk with a fatuously peaceful look was urinating contentedly against the embankment wall. Passing by, a neatly dressed middle-aged woman paused in stupefaction. She called out indignantly, "How vile! Isn't there one volunteer militiaman around here to take this hooligan into custody?" Her diction told Barkov that she was educated, her tone and manner that she was a Party member, and her several gold teeth that she could afford to pay for private dentistry.

The drunk turned. He, also, was middle-aged, largely bald, with rough-hewn features and the body of a man who does physical labour. "What's disgraceful?" he asked jovially, with a thickened tongue. "It's an act of nature, I had no place else to go. Don't you make pee-pee, comrade?"

Some of the men in the ice-cream line laughed, and the drunk flashed them an appreciative smile. He had about completed his business.

"Antisocial vermin like you ought to be sent to a camp!" the woman told him with disgust.

"Did you hear that – a *camp*?" the drunk asked with resentment as he fumbled with his trouser buttons. "When I went into Berlin and got my third medal, what wouldn't she have done for me?" He turned back to the woman. "You there – was I disgraceful when I pissed on Hitler's bunker?"

CHAPTER 2

"A filthy windbag like you never even saw the front lines," the woman replied with scorn. "If you'd won any medals, you'd be wearing them right now the way other men do."

"Can't wear what a bitch like you stole from me."

A militiaman appeared. He was in his mid-twenties, tall and slender, in his mouse-grey uniform, wearing white gloves and a white cap with a red band around it. The indignant woman whispered to him, pointing to the drunk, who immediately started off with an unsteady lurch. The militiaman caught up with him and took hold of his arm. "You'll have to come with me, comrade."

"I can't. Absolutely impossible."

"Why?" The question was asked patiently. "You're not too drunk to know that when a militiaman—"

"Can't!" the drunk interrupted. "It's hot, I'm going swimming."

"*That* I certainly won't let you do! Every year there are drunks who drown while swimming."

The woman spoke up. "Official figures show that alcohol accounts for more than two thirds of the crimes committed in our country."

"And for more than ninety-five per cent of the pissing," the drunk added with a grin.

At this the militiaman laughed, although he tried to hide it. The woman gave them both a withering glance and marched away.

"Now, be a good fellow," the drunk said. "You know what a sobering-up station for the night will mean – it'll cost me fifteen roubles... that's damn expensive."

By this time Barkov had his cup of ice cream and the little wooden stick that came with it. As he walked off, leaving the two in discussion, he reflected that this was a third item of bookkeeping: the friendly, helpful attitude of the police when neither politics nor serious crime were involved. Under the tsars, if a drunken working man had committed a nuisance on the embankment, he would have been thrown into a cell and beaten.

A little further on he paused beside a one-legged man of about fifty who was selling lottery tickets. The man had crutches under his arms, and his stump was above the knee level. Pinned on his shirt was the Order of the Red Star. Barkov bought ten tickets. The man said warmly, "Thanks, chum. I imagine you were at the front?"

Barkov nodded. "How is it you're not wearing an artificial leg?"

"I have one, but somehow I haven't gotten used to it." He grinned.

They shook hands, and Barkov went on, wondering if there was any country in the world where there were as many men with only one leg. Surely not.

This, too, had to be part of his bookkeeping. Three times in thirty-five years Russia had been invaded from the west. If the men in the Kremlin, gripped by a security neurosis, had jumpy nerves, it was not good. They could be erratic and make needless mistakes, but their behaviour required understanding as well as criticism. The books had to be kept intelligently, the columns added up – he couldn't weigh Viktor's teeth in a vacuum.

5

He left the embankment to take the subway to the hospital. Passing a food store, he paused to eat something. He purchased a quarter of a kilo of fried smelts for himself, and, for his wife, not only a jar of the Bulgarian plums she liked so much, but a novelty: a bottle of mango juice from India. Her diet was so restricted that he always was on the lookout for delicacies to please her.

Since there were no benches in the vicinity, he placed the anthology of poetry he was carrying on the kerbstone and sat down on it. Eating, he took a slip of paper from his back pocket. The key lines of a number of jokes were scribbled on it, and he began to jog his memory. These days he spent several hours a week telephoning friends for the latest political jokes, off-colour stories and whatnot. He fed them to Anna as though they were medicines.

"Daniil – Daniil Barkov? My Heavens, it *is* Daniil!" a voice boomed happily.

Barkov was stunned at the sight of the man beaming down at him. "Bulldog? Sanka?"

"Who else?"

Still holding a few smelts in the brown paper in which they had been wrapped, Barkov jumped to his feet with a cry. "The day after I was wounded someone from our platoon was brought into the hospital and said you'd been killed."

With a burst of laughter: "How dead do I look?"

They embraced strongly and kissed each other on the lips. Maretsky was a head taller then Barkov, a bear of a man tending now to obesity, but with the pugnacious jaw and heavy eyebrows that Barkov remembered so affectionately. He was wearing the Medal of Valour on his jacket.

"You look splendid – the same Bulldog."

"And I, of course, have seen your ugly mug in magazines so many times that I wasn't surprised at the grey hair. Except for that you look as lean and fit as when we were... oh, pardon, dear," he said to the stout, pretty woman beside him. "This is Valeriya, my wife. And this is Daniil Petrovich—"

"Don't you think I know?" she interrupted, extending her hand. "Sanka is very proud of you. We've both read every word you've published."

"Damn you, Bulldog," Barkov exclaimed almost angrily, "why didn't you get in touch with me through the Writers' Union?"

Maretsky shrugged with embarrassment. "I thought of it many times, but I'm not much of a letter writer – and, besides, I would say to myself that a man so well known must be very busy and wouldn't want to be bothered."

"How stupid!" Barkov punched him lightly on the arm. "After what we went through together?"

Maretsky suddenly guffawed. "That's right. We not only went through a lot, but we shared things." Tilting his head, he winked so that his wife wouldn't observe it.

The wink brought back memories that Barkov had tucked away with care. It would be impossible now for him to take a woman by force, but at the age of nineteen, after seeing with horror and fury the endless savageries perpetrated by the Germans in occupied Russia, he, like others, had said "*Frau... Komm*"* the moment he entered German soil. He asked quickly, "So, what's life like for you now?"

"Marvellous. We live in Kiev – a good apartment. I'm a foreman in a machine-tool plant. Valeriya is a bacteriologist, and we have three magnificent children – I'm not boasting at all." Laughter. "What about you, old friend?"

Barkov hesitated for a moment. "I don't have any children. My wife's health prevented it. In fact, she's in the hospital now."

Both Maretskys spoke at once expressing sympathy, asking what the illness was.

"Cirrhosis of the liver. It developed years ago, the result of malnutrition during the war."

"Oh, yes," said Maretsky's wife bitterly, "the damn Fritzes are still killing our people by secondary effects – hypertension—"

Maretsky interrupted his wife brusquely. "And you're remarkably careless in your choice of words, Valeriya. Why not consider Daniil's feelings before speaking of killing?"

Valeriya flushed and started to apologize, but Barkov interrupted her. "You didn't tell me anything I don't know. My wife's condition is irreversible."

"As bad as that? How long..." Maretsky sucked his thick lower lip with a distressed look.

"She may live several years or only a few months."

"I'm so sorry, Daniil."

CHAPTER 2

"Yes, it's abominable," Barkov replied openly. "Anna is a wonderful woman."

"In one of your early novels (was it *The Homecoming*?)," Maretsky asked, "you described a young soldier coming back from a hospital—"

"Yes, that was about Anna and myself."

"Such a touching, romantic story," Valeriya murmured. "I remember you described the girl as very lovely."

"Yes, before her illness advanced, Anna was stunning. Listen, I'm on my way to see her now. Could we meet later, or tomorrow?"

"We're going to the hotel to pack. We have to be at the airport in two hours."

"Damn you, Bulldog, I'll scarcely forgive you for never getting in touch with me. How often do you come to Moscow?"

"From now on I hope it'll be every several months. Our youngest, she's sixteen, is a cellist with so much talent that she's been accepted at the conservatory here. We came up to settle her with a relative. Give me your address. The next time I come, you'll know it."

As they were exchanging addresses, Barkov came to a sudden decision. "Sanka, there's something on my mind. Can you stay five minutes longer?"

"Why, yes. What is it?"

"I want your private opinion about something. We can trust each other not to gossip, eh?"

"Of course. And Valeriya as well."

Quietly, speaking as objectively as he could, Barkov described the demonstration he had witnessed. He tried not to convey his own feelings about it. When he had finished, he said, "So, I'd like to hear from both of you. What do you think of the demonstrators – and what's your opinion of how they were dealt with?"

"Disgusting!" Valeriya said immediately. Her round, pretty face was suddenly transformed by inner agitation. "For absolutely nothing my brother had to sit twelve years in a Mordovian camp. Now he's rehabilitated, but that doesn't give him new kidneys or pay him back for his horrible suffering. Wasn't there enough cruelty under Stalin? Are we going to slide back into the same snake pit? My God, I hope not."

"Keep your voice down, eh, Valeriya?" Maretsky cautioned, glancing around. "Beating them was wrong, of course. But they were certain to be arrested, weren't they?"

"Why? Do you remember Article 125 of the Constitution?"

"No."

"It gives citizens the right of freedom of speech and freedom to demonstrate."

"Yes, I remember now. But, Daniil, do you make it a habit to drink eyewash? Freedom to demonstrate has meant on national holidays like 7th November* and 1st May. It has never meant the right to oppose a decision of the Kremlin."

"That's how it's been, of course. But legally, according to the Constitution itself, shouldn't there be that right?"

"There should, perhaps, but I'm not naive. If—"

"And morally, Sanka?"

"Perhaps, yes, but morality didn't keep that poor slob from getting his teeth kicked out. He should have known in advance."

"But that's precisely what is still wrong and backward in our country, don't you see?" his wife burst out. "We—"

"Keep your voice down," Maretsky interrupted. "*Please!*"

She flashed a glance around and continued almost in a whisper, but with great intensity. "We know now that Stalin made a great many wrong decisions, terrible ones. Yet at the time no one could oppose anything he said or did. So what about the men in leadership now? Must they always be right in everything *today*, even though we'll be told *tomorrow* that they made blunders in this and that and so forth? Must we continue for ever to say 'Yes, Your Worship' the way our ancestors did under the tsars?"

CHAPTER 2

Maretsky smiled. "Valeriya, my dear, you and Daniil are perhaps correct morally, legally, politically, and in every way – except realistically."

"You don't mind going back to the snake pit?"

"It won't happen, the Stalin days are gone for ever. But—"

"Maybe, I hope so," his wife interrupted. "But, meanwhile, his shadow lies heavy over our whole country, and you know it!"

"And, meanwhile," Maretsky continued, "there's something else to bear in mind. To play the cello our Mayka doesn't need Article 125 of the Constitution. Her training at the conservatory won't cost us a rouble; her teachers will be the best in the world; she will be helped to go as far as her talent will take her. Our country is far from perfect, but I personally feel no need to improve things if it will mean getting my teeth kicked out." He turned to Barkov. "That's how you feel also, isn't it? Or else, why didn't you join the demonstrators?"

"There were reasons why I didn't join them, Sanka, but that has nothing to do with their right to demonstrate without being abused and arrested. Since I witnessed what happened to them, have I the moral right to keep silent?"

"Not only the right, but the necessity!" Maretsky replied strongly. "What are you going to do – send a letter about it to Western journalists the way that Solzhenitsyn does? Do you want to disgrace yourself giving ammunition to our enemies in the West?"

"But what about my brother's sufferings?" Valeriya asked her husband. "Have you forgotten what he said to us when he came back? He said that there were millions of dead eyes watching us from the grave – that we *all* had a moral duty to see that such injustice never occurred again."

Maretsky shrugged. "Injustice is as old as the human race. Is life as a whole better for us now than it was fifteen years ago... ten... five? Yes! That's my practical answer – don't buzz my head with poetry. And now, Daniil, I'm afraid we have to go."

Barkov nodded. He kissed Valeriya's hand, embraced Maretsky and said, "Look me up next time, damn you." But, as they parted, he thought with a sigh that Sanka would certainly not look him up when he became a Signer. And that was sad for him, for Sanka, and especially for their country.

Chapter 3

I

Barkov always enjoyed the walk from the subway station to the hospital. The Leningradsky Prospect, wider than a football field, had eight traffic lanes separated by a tree-shaded pedestrian walk. He liked the conceptual grandeur of the avenue, and felt that it must have been designed by someone like himself who had spent his childhood in the old Moscow with its many narrow lanes and wooden houses.

As he walked, the clamorous siren of an ambulance on emergency service came from behind him and then rushed ahead. It left him feeling as though a hand had reached into his chest and squeezed his heart. Not quite a month before he had been riding inside a similar ambulance with his stomach knotted and his pulse beating wildly as he stared at his pallid-faced wife, who was in a coma. In the last days of July, he and his wife had left their country home in the writers' colony of Peredelkino and driven into the city. Anna worked part-time for the Institute of World Economy and International Relations. Her superior was leaving for his month's vacation, and there were matters he needed to discuss about a book she was translating. When they arrived, she lay down to rest, while Barkov went out to shop. Since they had not been in the apartment for a month, it required two trips for him to get what they would need for their several days in Moscow. When he returned the second time, he was stunned to find Anna gaily sucking a leg bone of the broiled chicken he had bought. He burst out at her in instant reproach.

Anna's fragile state of health depended for its balance upon a diet so low in protein that Barkov had to eat his own meals out of her sight. For her sake, they never ate in a restaurant and never dined at the home of friends. At breakfast that morning. she had had most of her total allowance of protein for the day: two small slices of sturgeon and a piece of the black bread she loved. Often she found it more satisfying to eat her allotted twenty grams in one meal, preferring, as she put it, "one good chew to three nibbles". But consuming double her allowance was absolutely forbidden – it could be lethal – and Barkov cried out in distress, "How could you do it, Anna – how could you?"

Prokofiev's *Lieutenant Kijé** was playing on their hi-fi at the moment, and Anna waved the chicken bone as if it were a conductor's baton. She told him gaily that he had turned into a martinet, and she intended to look for another husband. The chicken had smelt so delicious that she couldn't resist sucking on a bone – but she had removed the meat before doing so. What was there to be so upset about?

Barkov sighed with relief and apologized for shouting. Half an hour later she was reading to him from a magazine as he dusted their books. When her reading began to slow down and she started to pause between phrases, he assumed that she was slipping off into a nap, something she did frequently. Turning, he saw that her eyes were half closed, and that she was leaning back against the chair. A few moments later, however, she muttered his name.

"What?" he asked, continuing to dust.

"Daniil?" she repeated again.

He walked over to her. "What is it?"

"I feel... strange."

"How do you mean?"

There was a pause before she answered. "Foggy..."

An alarm bell rang for Barkov. Her physician had warned that an inability to think clearly would be the result of toxic substances in her blood. Quickly he went into the kitchen, opened the refrigerator and pulled out the platter of chicken.

CHAPTER 3

A glance told him that she had lied: she had not cut away the leg meat. Worse, a portion of the breast also had been sliced off. He ran back to the living room to call their neighbourhood clinic for advice. With his hand on the telephone, he glanced at Anna. His jaw dropped, and he stood riveted. She was sitting up now, looking in his general direction with glassy eyes. Both her hands, upraised, seemed to be waving goodbye to him in a most bizarre fashion, flapping forward and back, forward and back, in a gross, exaggerated gesture.

"Anna," he cried, moving towards her. "What..."

Her hands flapped again, and she fell unconscious over the side of the chair. Barkov leapt to the phone and dialled emergency ambulance service. The calm voice of the woman who answered helped him keep hold of himself. She told him that there was a physician sitting beside her, and that if he would provide them quickly with the necessary information, the doctor would know what drugs and equipment to send in the ambulance, and how to prepare the hospital. She asked what the emergency was and told him to speak clearly.

"My wife just fainted. She has cirrhosis of the liver caused by malnutrition. She just ate more than double her allotment of protein."

"One moment." There was a ten-second pause. "Was she mentally clear before she fainted?"

"No, she felt foggy."

"...Did you notice any unusual movement of her hands?"

"Yes! Both hands flapped forward a number of times, as though she was waving goodbye to me."

"What is your address?"

After he had given it, the calm voice said, "An ambulance will be there within ten minutes."

Barkov knew about the emergency ambulance service, but had not had any experience with it. He was ready to weep with gratitude when a doctor and two male attendants with a stretcher came to his door in less than the ten minutes. The doctor, a woman in her thirties, did a number of things in rapid succession: she took Anna's pulse and blood pressure, listened to her heart and lungs, palpated her belly, smelt her breath. Then she directed the attendants to carry her down. Barkov, who had seen a TV documentary about this service, asked with indignation why she was not administering emergency treatment. The doctor explained that Anna was in a hepatic coma – the odour of her breath was uniquely characteristic, and the involuntary flapping of her hands was called "liver flap". A short wait for the treatment she needed would make no difference in her recovery. However, it could be done more efficiently in a hospital, since it involved the administration of neomycin both by enema and by a tube moved down her oesophagus into her stomach.

It was not until Barkov was pacing the waiting room that he realized how angry at Anna he was. Why had she done this to herself – and to him? A few hours later, when her physician spoke to him, his anger dissolved into understanding and pity.

What Anna had done, said Doctor Nikolayev, had been a familiar, almost inevitable rebellion against her illness and the terrible severity of her diet. Life actually was easier for someone in prison than it was for her. A prisoner was not called upon to exert constant willpower – locked doors and guards controlled every activity. But for Anna the awareness that food she craved was in the refrigerator made for a much more tense and difficult daily life. For a thousand days and nights since her last hospitalization she had kept her control – on the thousand and first, she had lost it.

Barkov was grateful for the explanation, but the prognosis for the future was devastating. Although Doctor Nikolayev was confident that Anna would emerge from her coma and would recover her mental faculties within a week, he was afraid – in fact, quite certain – that Anna never would return to her previous fragile but functioning state of health. From

CHAPTER 3

now on, she would remain physically weak, largely confined to bed. Moreover, despite the diuretics she would be given, it was likely that she would have some permanent swelling of her ankles and an accumulation of some water in her abdomen. At best she would have a few more years of life, provided she adhered without deviation to an even stricter regime: almost no salt, low intake of fluids, medicines as instructed, and the same miserable limit of twenty grams of protein. If she broke this discipline, she would die quickly.

That night, with this awful, unalterable verdict heavy on his heart, Barkov drank himself into a stupor. It was now some thirteen years since Anna's illness first had manifested itself. At their neighbourhood clinic they learnt that it was a familiar syndrome. The widespread malnutrition among civilians during the ghastly war years was the cause of many ailments. In Anna's case it was a diseased liver. With the aid of diet and medicines, her downhill slide was slow, yet inexorable. At first its only serious consequence was her inability to have children – she had a series of miscarriages. It grieved them, but since they loved each other devotedly, it bound them more closely together. For the past three years, however, she had become a semi-invalid, her vigour gone, her face thin and sickly-looking, her once-lovely body now unattractive.

Her illness crippled Barkov's life as well as her own. As the months passed, the idea of a secret relationship with another woman occurred to him more than once, but he found it impossible to do anything about it. His mind told him that it would not be a betrayal of Anna, but his heart knew he would feel a guilt that would corrode their relationship. Their lives had been intertwined from the time they had met at the age of sixteen, and they had had precious years together. He wanted nothing to mar what he still had with her.

Only a few days after she fell into her hepatic crisis, however, all changed. A friend of hers came from the Institute bearing flowers from her colleagues. Lidia Karpova had been elected because she and Anna had been members of a quartet that played baroque music. Barkov had not seen Lidia for some years, because he and Anna had moved to their country home after her last hospitalization. Lidia was an attractive woman. and she seemed especially so on this day when his poor Anna, skin yellow with jaundice, was still in a coma. Lidia was in her late thirties, bright-eyed and vibrant, unmarried like so many of her age group, whose potential husbands either had died in the war or were living out their crippled, unhappy lives in sanatoriums. She came visiting when Anna could not be seen, and when Barkov was in a depressed state. He had a need to talk to someone, but all of his close friends were away on vacation. The fact that he had met Lidia often over a good many years provided the sense that she was a friend, even though, in actuality, he did not know her well. But she was sympathetic, and there was, in addition, a caressing look in her eyes that he responded to without knowing he was doing so.

They left the hospital and walked for several hours. Barkov talked frankly of his love for Anna and of his aching sorrow over what had happened. He did not mention the frustration her illness had brought to his life, but there was no need for that: Lidia was an intelligent woman.

What Barkov did not know that afternoon was that side by side with her genuine sympathy for Anna there was an inevitable calculation going on in Lidia's mind and throbbing heart. Barkov had told her that Anna was condemned to die in a few months or years. Sooner or later he surely would get married again. Why not to her? She liked him and always had. She was desperately lonely – it was not something to leave to chance if she could help bring it about.

Lidia had a room-mate who also worked at the Institute, but she was away for the month of August. She asked Barkov up to her apartment for a bite of food. He was more than willing: the hours of talk had relieved his feelings considerably. Besides,

CHAPTER 3

he already was aware that he enjoyed being in the presence of this woman, and he was in no hurry to walk away from that caressing look. They stopped off at a foreign-currency store on the way, and he bought a bottle of Courvoisier and some Danish cheeses. Lidia had tasted Georgian brandy before, but never French cognac. She found it superb, and had no idea of its potency. Sipping it as they nibbled the cheeses, she became charmingly drunk. She had not had any specific idea beforehand of how she would try to grapple Barkov to her, but with her inhibitions lessened by the cognac, she suddenly, without willing it, said "Life is short, Daniil, so terribly short" and kissed him ardently. Her words spoke directly to his private anguish, her sensuous kiss to a strong need.

Later he spoke to her soberly, telling her that he would allow nothing to detract from the time and attention Anna would need when she came home from the hospital. Lidia touched his face gently and asked him to listen to her. She liked him enormously, but she was profoundly sorry for Anna and never would make any demands on him. The fact that they had enjoyed each other sexually didn't mean that they had made any commitments.

Lidia had spoken sincerely, and it was what Barkov needed to hear – but he stayed the night, and they met daily thereafter. Within two weeks they were discussing how they could spend some time together after Anna came home. Since Barkov carefully avoided the word "love", Lidia never told him that she had fallen as wildly and flutteringly in love with him as a teenage girl. And even when he told her how sad he was that Anna had not been able to have children, intuition advised her it would be a mistake to say she was only thirty-eight and might still bear a child. She would let him set the pace of their relationship.

Things were very good between them – the flow of emotion restrained to the degree that it needed to be, but very good nevertheless.

2

Entering the hospital, Barkov went to the cloakroom for the white gown visitors were required to wear. As he was putting it on, he noticed a large painting on a wall of the lobby. It had not been there on Friday. It was a reproduction of a famous scene: Lenin on a small platform addressing an outdoor mass meeting of workers and soldiers. Due to the fact that the centennial year of Lenin's birth was approaching, portraits of the great man, photographs and posters, sculptures small, large and gigantic, were appearing everywhere like forest mushrooms after a summer rain. Barkov found this monumental iconography a colossal bore. Although the official year had not yet begun, he already was weary of being confronted by Lenin's arresting face. In his opinion Lenin had been a very great man indeed, but why was it necessary to force-feed people as though they were geese on a French farm? Overfed geese might produce more pâté – overfed people simply ceased to respond.

Nevertheless, he found himself looking at the father of the Soviet people once again as he waited for the elevator (Lenin writing at his desk in the Kremlin), and still a third time (Lenin with a cat on his lap) when he passed the recreation room on the sixth floor, where ambulatory patients conversed, played chess, read newspapers and magazines.

He paused at the duty desk to enquire about Anna. The nurse told him that his wife was about the same physically, but had seemed somewhat depressed the day before. He frowned, thanked her and continued down the quiet hall. It was not a regular visiting hour, but Anna's physician considered his visits to be therapeutic – he could come at any time and remain as long as she wished him to.

He peered into the three-bed ward – a bright, cheerful room. Anna's was the farthest bed from the doorway, near the open window, and he couldn't tell whether she was asleep. Her eyes

CHAPTER 3

were closed, but she had a small radio on her chest with the hearing plug in her ear.

Since music helped the tedious hours go by, he had bought her a Japanese transistor radio in a foreign-currency store. He nodded and smiled as he tiptoed past the two other women. Quietly he put the book and the two bottles he was carrying on the stand by Anna's bed. Her eyes opened at once. She smiled, turned off the radio and removed the plug from her ear. "Hello, darling. I'm glad your throat is better."

The sore throat had been his excuse for not visiting the day before. The letter from his Polish friend, Shika, had been so devastating that he knew he could not see Anna without communicating his distress.

"You came just as a record ended," Anna continued. "It was the Borodin* playing one of the late Beethoven* quartets. What marvellous musicians they are!"

Her voice always had been soft – he had called it fondly "her seductive contralto" – but now it sometimes was a bit difficult for him to hear all of her words. It pained him to have to strain to listen to her – as it pained him to see her as she was now. The luminous beauty of her grey eyes had faded. Her skin was jaundiced, her bone-thin face looked twenty years older than her age, the cords of her once-lovely (so often kissed) neck were now sadly visible.

"Ah, you brought me some plums. Thank you. What's in the other jar?"

"Mango juice from India. Would you like to taste it?"

"Yes, please."

"How are you feeling today?"

"Perhaps a little stronger."

She found the juice delicious, and he told her that from now on he would be on the lookout for it. Anna turned on her side so that they could talk without being overheard. She held out her right hand. "I have something to tell you, Daniil. Hold my hand, dear."

He sat down and took her hand in both of his. The sight of the silver ring against the yellowish skin of her finger brought a lump to his throat.

"Yesterday I asked Doctor Nikolayev to tell me frankly what my future was going to be." The tired voice died away for a few moments. "I know everything."

Barkov nodded and swallowed. There was a kind of serenity in her manner that astonished him.

"So there won't be any lying between us, dear, will there? I'm going to speak from my heart. I want you to do the same."

He remained silent with his jaw muscles working. Although he didn't know what she was going to say, he felt awful. One way or another, they were going to talk about her death.

"I've made a decision. If daily living ever becomes too disagreeable, I am not going to linger on. It'll be simple for me to have a magnificent last banquet. I'll stuff myself with sausage, bread, caviar and champagne and depart peacefully." She smiled in a way that made him realize she was genuinely amused by the notion of such a death. "However, the way I am now I have no pain, merely weakness. So I'd like to live my life out to the full. Even the act of dying is a part of life, don't you think? Even feeling depressed sometimes, and sorry for oneself. A person passes through this world only once, so why cut it short unless you have to?"

He rubbed his nose and nodded.

She smiled again, but this time it was a wan smile and she spoke more slowly. "I won't deny... I have fantasies. This morning I found myself wishing... we could go to Obraztsov's puppet theatre* once more and see that delicious satire on Hollywood...* and then go home... have some herring and wine... make sweet love again the way we used to..." Her voice trailed off, and she looked away from him for a few moments.

Barkov stroked her hand. He felt like weeping, and told himself that he absolutely must not, that it would be cruel to burden her with his own heartache.

CHAPTER 3

Anna turned back to him. "Obviously, I can never be even half a wife to you again. Shhh... don't!" she interrupted as he began to speak. "You'll really wound me if you lie, Daniil."

"I wasn't going to lie."

"Good. But hear me out before you say anything."

He nodded.

"I've made a decision, dear. When I leave the hospital, I'm going to a sanatorium. I know you'll come to visit me – I take that for granted. But it'll make me feel terribly guilty to keep you tied to a marriage that's inadequate for you. I'll be much happier if we establish a new relationship on a realistic basis." She drew a deep breath and sighed aloud. "Well, I've told you."

Barkov kissed her hand and rubbed it against his cheek. When he spoke, his voice was quiet, but a bit hoarse, because of the intensity of his feelings. "I'm glad you talked openly. Now I'll ask you a question. Let's pretend this cirrhosis never had developed, but that I was the one who was ill... in a hospital right now after a stroke. And let's say the physicians told us there was no hope of a good recovery, that I would be an invalid in a wheelchair for the rest of my life, unable to walk or speak normally, and so on. Would you want me to go to a sanatorium?"

She turned her eyes away from his.

"Answer me honestly, Anna."

The silence lengthened. He moved one hand to her cheek and gently turned her head so that she was facing him again. "Anna?"

She sighed. "No, I wouldn't."

"Why not?"

The answer came reluctantly. "I couldn't bear to be separated from you even if you were an invalid."

"Then why," he asked softly, "do you insult me? Why don't you credit me with as much feeling for you? My heart, my whole being, are so tied to you that I don't want to lose your presence in my life one day sooner than necessary."

She gazed at him, searching his face. Her lips were trembling.

"You're my Anna, my heart's love," he whispered. "Whatever we can have together, I want."

He bent lower and kissed the trembling lips which clung to his. He felt his heart pounding from the intensity of his love and sorrow.

A few moments later a nurse came in with a bedpan for one of the other women. He welcomed the interruption and left the room.

3

"Some more juice?" he asked.

"Not yet. Were you able to work yesterday?"

The prepared lie spoke itself easily. "I had a very good day – four pages." He gestured slightly, and his lips formed the word "music". Anna nodded and said, "I think there might be some music on now. Do you mind while we talk?" She reached for the radio.

"Of course not," he replied in dialogue familiar to both of them.

She tuned in a Sibelius* symphony. With the proper words having been spoken in case there were microphones in the room, Barkov began to whisper beneath the music. "Philemon told me a story about an important bureaucrat who was travelling by auto in Georgia and got lost. He saw an old peasant and asked how to get to the main road to Batumi.* The peasant didn't know. The bureaucrat then enquired where the main road was to the capital. The peasant asked: 'What capital?' 'Tiflis,'* the bureaucrat shouted. 'Tiflis.' The peasant said he didn't know. In a great temper, the bureaucrat yelled, 'You don't know very much about anything, do you?' The peasant replied, 'No, but I'm not lost.'"

Anna smiled, and he felt pleased.

CHAPTER 3

"Ilya Krasny called last night. He and Veronika just returned from their vacation. They send their love, and want to know when they can visit you."

"I look so awful I hate the idea of their seeing me."

"Anna! Old friends like them?"

She sighed, and the wan smile came to her face again. "Yes, how foolish... Vanity, vanity! Tell them to come."

"Good, you need company. Now, I have a real beauty for you. A woman is putting her grandchild to bed. She gives him a drink of water, a goodnight kiss, and goes out of the room. A minute later the child calls, 'Babooshka?'

"'What is it?'

"'Was Stalin a good man?'

"'You know sleep time is not question time. No, Stalin was a bad man. Now, I don't want to hear any more from you, darling. Go to sleep.'

"A minute later there's another call. 'Babooshka?'

"'No more questions.'

"'But I need to know. Was Lenin a good man?'

"'Yes, Lenin was a good man. Now, that's absolutely the last question I'll answer. Go to sleep!'

"After another minute: 'Babooshka.'

"'I'm not answering any more questions!'

"'But Party Secretary Brezhnev* – is Comrade Brezhnev a good man?'

"'Go to sleep, I told you, go to sleep. When he's dead, we'll know.'"

Anna didn't laugh or even smile. She drew a quick breath and exclaimed, "Oh, my goodness, that cuts like a knife! It's so true it hurts."

Barkov nodded. "I imagine it's being whispered in every city in the country."

"Did someone actually tell it to you over the phone?"

"No, of course not. When I left here on Friday, I met Lelka outside the hospital. Khristian is in here."

"What's wrong with him?"

"Minor surgery. He's fine."

Anna's eyes flicked to the other women. The younger one was sleeping, the older still knitting. "What's the news on Czechoslovakia?"

An acid note came into Barkov's voice. "To protect us against capitalist lies, the Kremlin has started jamming foreign radio broadcasts." The crimson teeth, wrapped in a handkerchief in his pocket, suddenly felt like weights. "Anna," he whispered, "I saw something shocking today. Would you mind hearing about it?"

"Tell me."

He described the demonstration. She was silent as she listened, although her face mirrored some of her feelings, and she remained silent afterwards.

"No comment?"

"It's sickening... Just dreadful." She paused. "Was there anyone you knew among the spectators?"

"Sandler."

"Anyone else?"

"No."

She hesitated, looking at him closely.

"What is it?"

"If the demonstrators are held for trial, the official version of what happened won't be the truth."

"Naturally not."

"Why don't *you* write a true account, Daniil? And start circulating typewritten copies *before* the trial?"

The suggestion was so unexpected it left Barkov tongue-tied.

"You're surprised, I know," Anna whispered. "Now, I'll admit something I'm not ashamed of. Eight years ago, when the first diagnosis of my cirrhosis was made, Doctor Nikolayev advised me that the more tranquil a life I could lead, the better. I knew without his saying, so that he must have told you the same. He did, didn't he?"

CHAPTER 3

Barkov nodded.

"Isn't that why you've kept silent about events that made you furious – like the various trials that others were protesting?"

Barkov nodded again and began to stroke her hand.

"I never said anything because I wanted so much to stay as healthy as possible. I was afraid that if you got involved it would lead to all sorts of tensions – struggles in the Writers' Union, bitter debates with some of our friends, the KGB snooping around us... But I have no reason to be selfish any more. If I die a few months sooner, what's the difference? The only one to consider now is you. If you want to take a public stand, do it."

Barkov started to speak, hesitated, then remained silent.

Anna smiled. "Daniil, don't you think I know you by now? A little while ago you asked me not to insult you. Now I'll ask you the same."

Barkov whispered, "Thank you, Anna, dearest. What happened today ought to be told as widely as possible."

"And no one will doubt your word!" Anna added with a gleam of excitement coming into her tired eyes. "If you type up a few copies and give them to friends, other copies will multiply so rapidly that thousands of people will read it within a month. It might even prevent the demonstrators from being put on trial."

"And if they *are* put on trial, the defence will surely call me as a witness."

"Does the thought of that worry you?"

"No, I'd welcome it! There are too many dead eyes watching from the grave," he added, repeating what Valeriya Maretsky had said. "Anyone in my position has a duty to speak out. If I were a physicist like Litvinov, it would take courage. But I don't work at an institute – I can't be dismissed from my post. And I have enough money to live for a long time without earning anything."

"There's one way they can make trouble for you – on the new book. The censors won't pass it for publication."

"So to hell with them. I'll circulate it in manuscript form. Thousands have read Solzhenitsyn's novels that way, haven't they?" He laughed lightly. "Self-publishing is probably the fastest-growing industry in the Soviet Union."

"Anyway," Anna observed, "we can thank our stars that these aren't the Stalin days. You won't get shot."

"I want very much to write it, Anna. We're in a critical period. The more of us who protest violations of the Constitution, the better the chance of achieving some reforms."

"Write it, I'll be proud of you!"

4

When Barkov was out on the street, he thought with an aching heart of the orphaned boy and elderly woman with whom Anna, for several months at different times during the war, had shared rations. Both had lost their identity and food cards. In the chaotic conditions of the time, it had not been easy to get new ones. If she hadn't shared her rations with them, she might not have developed her cirrhosis. Yet, if she had not done so, she would not have been Anna.

Chapter 4

I

Rain clouds were dark in the sky when Barkov arrived at Lidia's apartment house in the late afternoon. On the way from the hospital, he had stepped into a foreign-currency shop to buy several bottles of Courvoisier. He had nipped at one of them while the taxi took him to Kutuzovsky Prospect. Despite the sadness he had felt when he was with Anna, another person was in the forefront of his consciousness now: his Polish friend, Shika. He was on fire about Shika, and was impatient to tell Lidia about him. She had been out of the city several days for the wedding of a niece. Although she had called that morning to let him know she was home, he had not wanted to speak about Shika on the phone.

The six-storey apartment house in which Lidia lived was exactly like Barkov's, and less than a kilometre away from it. Nine years before, the buildings on both sides of the wide avenue had been constructed with unusual rapidity by means of prefabricated units. Since the quality of the mortar and paint used in finishing the buildings had been third-rate, they rapidly took on a shabby appearance both inside and out. Nevertheless, the apartments were private, basically sturdy, and therefore highly desirable compared to older housing. Some of them had been allotted to the construction workers who built them, but many had been assigned to Moscow's elite, and not a few to technicians like Lidia, who did skilled work in one of the institutes connected with the Academy of Sciences. Although her apartment was on the fifth floor in the rear and Barkov's on the second in front, they were exactly alike.

To Barkov's pleasure, the elevator, which had stopped running in midweek, was functioning again. He was glad to avoid the stairs on so warm and humid an afternoon. Lidia had found an antique brass knocker for her apartment door, and, before he struck it a second time, he was looking at her smiling face. She was a small, attractive, animated woman with jet-black, almond-shaped eyes and dark-brown hair that she wore in a ponytail. She always joked about her eyes, saying that a Tartar must have slipped between the thighs of one of her forebears, but she knew they were attractive and used black liner to enhance them. Despite the heat, she appeared fresh and cool in her Japanese kimono. The expression on Barkov's face, and his perfunctory kiss, told her he was distressed about something.

She closed the kimono over her breasts and gazed at him enquiringly as he moved into her small living-dining room. Colourful prints on the walls, and some hand-woven textiles thrown over the heavy furniture, made the room rather attractive.

"How was the wedding?" he asked, without being really interested.

"You know what those six-minute official weddings are like. But the family celebration afterwards was warm and happy. You look disturbed. Is it Anna?"

He decided that he didn't want to talk about Anna at this time, and he answered, "No, she's about the same. But several damn ugly things happened while you were gone." He put the bottles of cognac on the table. "Will you get me a glass?"

As Lidia left for the kitchen, he stepped out on the small balcony. In the distance were the upper storeys of one of Stalin's architectural legacies: the Hotel Ukraina, a monumental wedding-cake structure gleaming stark white against the dark clouds. Down below there was a good-sized rectangle of patchy lawn with people on benches around its sides and young children hard at work on swings. It was a peaceful scene,

CHAPTER 4

a normal Sunday afternoon in summer. He wondered what was being done to the eight demonstrators at the police station.

Lidia returned with two glasses and a plate of sliced smoked eel, a snack he loved. As they sat down opposite each other, she told him she didn't want anything to drink for the moment. She moistened the cardboard tip of a cigarette, lit it and waited with caressing eyes for him to talk. He filled a third of his glass, took a sip and then, on impulse, pulled the blue handkerchief from his pocket. He put it on the table between them and opened it.

"Heavens!" she exclaimed with a frown. "What are those? They look like teeth."

Barkov became sharply aware of something. It was the third time since noon that he would be describing the demonstration. He had known in advance how Anna would react. He had not known about the Maretskys, but had not cared. He realized now that he was acutely concerned about Lidia's response, but could not be certain what it would be. In their weeks together, their conversation had leant to the personal more than the political. And even though she had been distressed by the initial news of the invasion, she had been three days in another environment. For all he knew, her brother was a Party member, and she might have been overwhelmed by him and by the tidal wave of propaganda in the media. He riveted his eyes on her face as he told her what had happened in front of Execution Ground.

"How dreadful!" she exclaimed with strong feeling the moment he finished. And then, echoing his own thought, "And how sad for our country that eight demonstrators with their little banners have to be treated as though they're counter-revolutionaries with machine guns."

Barkov jumped up, went around the table and flung his arms around her. He kissed her repeatedly. "Thank you for that, thank you!"

She looked at him with a fond, slightly mocking smile. "This is the first time I've been kissed for a political reason."

He answered with a grin. "Don't you know the world we live in? Politics can divide people as well as nations."*

"Were you worried I'd react like a Stalinist? Don't you know me better by now?"

"Not altogether, no. There's a lot we don't know about each other."

"Well, bury your doubt in that area. But why did you pick up those teeth?"

Barkov sat down and took a sip of cognac. "For the same reason, I suppose, that in visiting Auschwitz I took away with me a child's spoon and fork. There was a pile of them near the ruins of the crematoria. I didn't want ever to forget the millions who were murdered in those gas chambers. The spoon and fork of a little child, such a little spoon and fork. I made a shadow box and put them inside."

"Are you going to frame those teeth?"

He folded the handkerchief and put it back in his pocket. "I don't know what I'll do with them." He took a deep breath. "Now, I want to talk about something else. I received a letter yesterday from Warsaw. Reading it was like getting kicked in the solar plexus."

"I'm sorry, Daniil."

He got up and began to pace the room, glass in hand. "Last week I told you I was worried about a Polish friend of mine, Shika Botwin, but I didn't go into the reasons."

"I remember. Was the letter from him?"

"Yes. Of the men I've known in my life, the one I love and admire most – aside from my father – is Shika. When I met him, he was a lieutenant in a Polish division attached to our army. Both of us were wounded in the street fighting in Breslau,* and ended up side by side in a hospital. He's ten years older than I am, so at that time he was almost thirty. He had the face of a pixie with sparkling blue eyes and flaming red hair. Even though he was thin and small, he was made of iron. He had been two years in Spain as

CHAPTER 4

a front-line soldier in the International Brigades,* and had been wounded twice there and then three times with us. He not only had a Medal of Valour, which was handed out to a lot of soldiers like myself, but he had the Order of the Patriotic War." Barkov speared a piece of the smoked eel, raised it to his mouth, then put it down again. He resumed pacing. "Shika had the merriest temperament of any man I've ever known. He was intellectually brilliant, and so well read that I was astonished to learn he'd only had a few years of schooling. He'd been working since he was twelve for his father, a candle-maker."

"Where did they live?"

"Cracow." Barkov drained his glass and poured it full again. There was a clap of thunder, and they both turned to look outside. A stir of breeze came into the room, and a few thick drops spattered against the open double windows.

"Ah, good," Lidia murmured. She lit another cigarette.

"Shika left the hospital before I did. Naturally, we assumed we'd never meet again. But not long after my first book began to be serialized – that was in '48 – he wrote me a letter in care of *Novy Mir** which was printing the stories. I was so excited and happy to know he was alive that Anna and I went to see him in Warsaw. At that time he was a major in the Polish army – later he became a colonel. Since then we've not only corresponded and talked on the telephone, but we've had six visits in the twenty years. He's stayed more than once at our home in Peredelkino."

"Is he a Party member?"

"Yes – from the time he was sixteen. But in private conversation there's nothing doctrinaire in his thinking."

"Married?"

"His wife died two years ago."

"Any children?"

"Two."

"Why did his letter upset you so much?"

There was another roll of thunder outside, and a burst of heavy rain. A flow of cool air began to enter the room. Barkov tossed off half the cognac in his glass and began to speak rapidly. His face had become flushed with both emotion and drink, and there was a blaze in his deep-set eyes. "In the middle of March I realized that Shika hadn't answered two letters I had sent him. I telephoned and found that his number had been disconnected. I cabled, and there was no answer. I applied for a visa to go to Warsaw – for the first time it was refused. I asked why. The clerk didn't know. I asked to see the ambassador. He was indisposed, and would call me when he felt better. He never called, and I never could see anyone in authority at the embassy."

"Has Shika been ill?"

"I wish he had been – he'd be suffering less than he is. In March he was summarily dismissed from the army. Why? Because he's a Jew! For no other reason!"

"That can't be, Daniil – Poland is a socialist country."

"Shika doesn't lie! There hasn't been a single word in our press of what he told me in his letter. In March of this year there were violent student riots in Warsaw and many other cities. Did you read or hear anything about them?"

"No."

"Neither did I. So what did the Polish government do? It blamed Zionists – read Jews – for instigating them. If it weren't so heartbreaking, it would be farce. Shika told me long ago that there were only about thirty thousand Jews in the whole country, most of them dedicated Communists like him. But the government came up with a Hitlerian lie to explain dissatisfaction among the students. Since March an organized expulsion of Jews has been going on in all areas of Polish life – education, journalism, science – on the ground that every Jew is a secret Zionist, and therefore a danger to the security of the state... no proof needed. Moreover, all Jews are free to leave the country – as more than half of them already have

CHAPTER 4

– provided they name Israel as the country to which they are emigrating."

Barkov drank off his glass of cognac as though it were lemonade. "Shika was thrown into such a deep depression that he couldn't pick up a pen to write to me. What finally got him to write is the fact that a former army colleague told him his division had received orders to move up to the Czech frontier. Shika's letter is a cry of pain and rage. The Soviet government is so alert to the alleged danger of Czechoslovakia slipping into the hands of fascists, but why is it unconcerned about this fascist treatment of Polish Jews?" Barkov hit his right fist hard against the palm of his left hand. "Shika's two boys were expelled from Warsaw University and have already left the country. But Shika won't sign an emigration application, because he refuses to support the lie that he's a secret Zionist. He's blacklisted for other work, and the pension they've given him is so miserable that he's already drawing on his savings. Short of actual physical murder, he's been assassinated."

Lidia said softly, "He's lost his wife, his sons, his work, his country – is there anything left to him?"

"Yes – his belief in socialism! He insists that the corruption of the Polish leadership is the cause of what has happened, not socialism itself."

"It would be so good if you could visit him now."

"Since I can't, I asked him to apply for a Soviet visa. I would like him to have a long visit with me if the Polish authorities will allow it. And I'm going to find out if I can send him any money." Barkov's voice rose. "In addition, I'm going to circulate a document about him. From one end of this country to the other people are going to read what happened to a Pole who earned the Soviet Order of the Patriotic War! And I'm also going to write an eyewitness report of what happened on Red Square this morning!"

"Daniil, you're very angry and a bit drunk – I don't think you realize what you just said."

"I'm not at all drunk! What's wrong with what I said?"

"I want to discuss your tactics. If—"

"I'll tell you what my tactics will be," he interrupted. "I'll take them from Solzhenitsyn, one of the moral giants of our century. I don't agree with every idea he has, but with the main principle... *yes*: full and open disclosure in the face of hypocrisy – the truth, the absolute truth, thrown into the mugs of opportunists and gangsters pretending to be Communists!"

"Fine, but one question: will what you write be published?"

"Of course not. But I'll act correctly. I'll submit my report in a normal manner to a number of newspapers and magazines. Then, after it has been rejected, I'll circulate the manuscript myself."

"With your name on it?"

"Of course! It will lose most of its effectiveness if my name isn't on it. In fact, I think I'll deliver it in person to the editorial department of *Pravda*."

"Daniil, don't tell me the demonstration this morning was smothered by accident?"

"Of course not."

"Or that the KGB agents will be dismissed for improper conduct?"

He became impatient. "Why these questions when the answers are obvious?"

"Because there's going to be a chain reaction when you present your eyewitness report to *Pravda*. Within half an hour news of it will travel to the Writers' Union, to members of the Central Committee, to the KGB. I don't think the authorities will take kindly to it: I think they will be very angry at your joining the ranks of the dissidents. What will happen then when you ask permission to send money to Shika?"

Barkov caught his breath.

"And what will happen when he goes to our embassy in Warsaw and asks for a visa to visit you? The request will be passed on to Moscow, where you, in the mean time, have become known as the author of 'Eyewitness Report'. Do you think Shika will get his visa?"

Barkov drank and remained silent.

"And if you also write about the sordid events in Poland and put your name on the document, you can be sure there will be no travel permits either way. You and Shika will never see each other again. Even your correspondence will be interfered with."

"You and your analytical mind," Barkov muttered with dismay.

"I see no reason why you can't write an anonymous account of the demonstration," Lidia continued. "However, you may have been photographed on Red Square. I suggest you don't use your own typewriter or Anna's. I have a new one on which I've only written a few letters. The KGB is not likely to identify anything typed on that."

There was a long silence. Barkov then said slowly, "I've just been having a telepathic conversation with Shika. You know what he told me? He said, 'Forget about sending me money, forget about our seeing each other. There are times when silence is a sin. Write what you ought to write and put your name on it!'" He sat thinking for a few moments more, then stood up slowly. "Now I don't want to talk any more about poor Shika. It hurts too much. Excuse me."

As he started to walk out of the room, he lost his balance and lurched heavily to one side. He recovered and was grinning at Lidia by the time she reached him. "Since you work in the field of statistics, madam, I ask you to observe with your mathematical eye how steadily and with what discipline I march towards the toilet. I am a soldier who has just received his two hundred grams of vodka before an attack."

Lidia followed him out of the room and across the minuscule foyer. She laughed and said "Bravo" when he entered the small cabinet. She continued on into the kitchen.

2

It had stopped raining, and the room was pleasantly cool. Fifteen minutes earlier Lidia had brought out the supper she had purchased in an expensive, ready-to-serve food store. She herself was eating heartily, but Barkov was only nibbling at the food while continuing to drink. The bottle of Courvoisier was two-thirds empty. His voice had become thick, and his mood had changed. He was describing with enthusiasm a project he had in mind – a documentary film about Vietnam. He wanted to follow the travels of a hand grenade from the time it was manufactured in the Soviet Union until it finally was hurled at the enemy by a Viet Cong soldier. If not for Anna's illness, he would be walking the Ho Chi Minh trail* right now.

Lidia's face and body became tight. "I hope you're never able to make the film. Just the other day you said survival in war is ninety per cent luck. You're too important a writer to risk your life making a documentary."

Barkov smiled at her. "To you I may be... an important writer... fine. But in the history of literature... I'm so far... a minor Russian writer of the twentieth..." His tongue twisted over the word, and he repeated it. "Twentieth century. We'll see if I do better in... the years ahead. And now I need to go to sleep."

Pushing up from his chair, he fell forward heavily on his hands and knees. He burst into laughter. "I knew I was a little drunk, but now I think... I'm drunker than I thought."

Lidia knelt by his side and put an arm around him. "Let me help you up."

Barkov laughed. "I weigh... eighty-two kilos, Lidochka. You try to help me up you'll... get a hernia. Do women get hernias?"

"What shall we do?"

"I have an idea... very creative." He moved his hands forward and sprawled at full length. "Sleep right here... comfortable floor. Give me a kiss, Lidochka." His eyes were already closed.

CHAPTER 4

She lay down beside him and kissed his cheek and one side of his lips.

"Lidochka, Lidochka... you're only thirty... what?"

"Eight."

"You seem strong and healthy. Are you?"

"Yes."

"Do you want... to have a child with me... a lovely, beautiful child?"

"Ask me tomorrow."

"*In vino veritas.** I'm asking... *in vino veritas*, Lidochka."

"Tomorrow you won't even remember this."

"Yes, I will."

He was quiet for a few moments, and then began to snore gently. Lidia lay for a while with her arm around him and her cheek pressed to his. Then she got up, put some records on her hi-fi and began to put away the food. Her cheeks were flushed at the thought of what he had said.

Chapter 5

I

The light was bright when Barkov awakened. His dry mouth and thirst helped him recall the evening before. He saw the expected note from Lidia on the small table in the kitchen, but he had to gulp a glass of water before reading it.

> Esteemed Minor Writer: I am free this evening. Are you? Please call me before lunch. Do you remember what you asked me before you fell asleep?
>
> L.

He drank another glass of water and wondered what he had asked. He also couldn't recall talking to her about minor writers.

He opened the small refrigerator and began to pull out the leftovers of the previous night's supper. He ate a slice of veal as he put water on the stove for tea. He went into the living room to use the telephone. He first asked for the time, and found that it was 7.55. He guessed that he had slept eleven or twelve hours. He called the hospital, and was told that Anna's condition was stable. He asked that a message be conveyed: he would visit about four in the afternoon. He chose that hour because he wanted sufficient time to write his eyewitness report, revise it, type it and take it to the editorial office of *Pravda*.

Eating his breakfast, he reread Lidia's note and tried again without success to recall what question he had asked her. Just thinking about her these days filled him with warmth and tenderness. The more he saw of her, the more attractive she became to him – a good companion, bright and mature, with the sparkle of some of the lusty women Frans Hals* had painted. He began to wonder if she still was able to bear. She was not yet forty, and he knew two women who had had children at forty-one and forty-three. It made him feel a traitor to Anna to dwell on this, and yet he wouldn't lie to himself: he always had felt deprived that she couldn't have children. He had been willing to adopt a child, but she never wanted to. How many times he had wished that Fate had treated her better! What joy if they could have had children and lived out full lives with each other!

It was cloudy outside, but warmer than the day before. Despite the humidity, he enjoyed the ten-minute walk from Lidia's apartment house to his own. He paused on the way to buy copies of *Pravda* and *Izvestia*. The latter reported angrily that counter-revolutionary Czechs were putting up anti-Soviet posters in Prague. It described them as having been drawn "with the saliva of mad dogs". ("Great style... superb metaphor," he thought.) He saw no mention in either paper of yesterday's demonstration on Red Square.

At the door to his apartment he looked in his mailbox, even though it was too early for the morning postal delivery, but no one had left a note. As he got out his keys to open the three padlocks by which his door was secured to the casing next to it, he realized that once again he had forgotten to ask Lidia why she didn't have padlocks on her door. It was no secret that there were only two or three types of door locks in Moscow, and that keys for any of them could be freely purchased. If Lidia's district had escaped thievery so far, it was not likely to do so much longer.

His apartment was stuffy, and he walked through the rooms opening the windows. His telephone rang. When he answered it, there was a click as the connection was broken off at the other end. He shrugged and went into the bathroom. He shaved and showered quickly, put on fresh clothes and called Lidia. She

CHAPTER 5

was in conference, and they spoke briefly, arranging to meet in the lobby of the Hotel Ukraina at seven. He did ask what the question was she had referred to in her note. She laughed and told him that she would wait to see if it came to his mind when he was sober.

He went to his desk at once, carrying a saucer on which he had placed the two teeth he had picked up on Execution Ground. Out of an undefined but strong feeling, he wanted to be able to eye them while he wrote his report. On the desk was Shika's ten-page letter, the handwriting large, hurried, with words crossed out and many insertions. Barkov put the saucer down on the letter and thought with deep anger that Shika, too, had had his teeth kicked out. In the months ahead he would have to find someone trustworthy who was travelling to Poland for an academic or scientific conference. He could carry a personal message to Shika, and, if a transfer of currency could be arranged, a sum of money also.

He heard something and turned towards his front door, listening. He heard it again – two quick taps. Since he didn't expect anyone, he assumed it would be Sandler, full of eagerness and enquiry. When he opened the door, he was astonished. His friend, Ilya Krasny, was standing with his left forefinger pressed to his lips to indicate a need for silence. His face looked very strained and anxious. He was holding a ballpoint pen in his right hand – presumably he had tapped on the door with it. Barkov stepped back and gestured for him to enter. After he did so, Barkov quickly looked out into the corridor – it was empty. He returned to the living room, where Krasny – still with his forefinger to his lips, was now pointing with the pen towards Barkov's hi-fi set. He made a circling gesture to indicate that he wanted Barkov to play a record. The suggestion that his apartment might be bugged was surprising to Barkov, but he did what his friend wanted. As they waited for the record to drop, Barkov held out his hand. Krasny wiped his palm on his trousers, but it was still moist when they shook hands.

THE EYEWITNESS REPORT

Krasny was a bit taller and more slender than Barkov, a distinguished-looking man with chiselled features, thinning brown hair and a thick moustache. Although they had talked on the phone on Saturday night, they had not seen each other in over a month, because Krasny and his wife had been in Bulgaria at a seaside resort. The moment the music began, they sat down side by side on the sofa and started to speak rapidly, in whispers.

"What's happened?" Barkov asked immediately. "And do you seriously think my apartment is bugged?"

"I doubt it. But I want to be absolutely certain we're not overheard." Krasny wet his lips quickly with his tongue. "I was the one who phoned you about twenty minutes ago and hung up when you answered. I've been calling you constantly from a neighbour's apartment since yesterday noon. I'm afraid my phone is being tapped."

"I was out all day, and I didn't sleep here last night. What's upset you so much?"

"We flew in from Sofia on Saturday afternoon. Eleven o'clock Sunday morning there was a knock on my door. At first I was delighted. It was Julius, my pilot, you've heard me talk about him, I haven't seen him for fifteen years. After half an hour of reminiscing he told me he had a purpose in coming to see me, it wasn't just social." Krasny's tongue flicked his lips. "The son of a bitch is a colonel in the KGB – he showed me his identity card. He's been living in Moscow for six months, but didn't look me up because of my membership in the Human Rights Committee. And that's what he came to talk about. He made it very plain he was doing me a favour, because I'd been his navigator and he liked me. If not for that, I would have been summoned officially to KGB headquarters."

"For what reason?"

"My activities as a citizen." Krasny had interlocked the fingers of both hands and was rubbing them together in an agitated manner. "He gave it to me straight. If I didn't stop

CHAPTER 5

my public activities, I'd be dismissed from my post at the university. Furthermore, I'd be barred from all research and from teaching anywhere at any level."

"Damn bastards!" Barkov whispered. "They can't arrest you, because you haven't broken the law, but they'll bar you from working the way they did Pavel Litvinov."

"That was the threat. Until they carry it out there's no way of knowing if they mean it."

"But meanwhile you walk a tightrope."

"Exactly! I didn't sleep at all last night. I said to him, 'Julius, this is all so stupid. I believe in socialism with my whole heart. Why am I being treated like an enemy?' Julius's police mentality revealed itself then. He looked at me in a very condescending way – the bureaucrat sure of his position and power – and replied, 'Stop your public activities, and then we'll know you believe in socialism!'" Krasny shook his head. "How degrading it is! I am to be told by a policeman what proper socialist behaviour is!"

"What are you going to do?"

"I don't know – and that's even more degrading. If you want to work, stop thinking – what a choice! I'm not going to be the only one they threaten like that. It was clear from what he said that this is the result of the events in Czechoslovakia. The KGB isn't acting on its own. The Kremlin doesn't like what developed there, so it intends to crack the whip more sharply at home."

"Did you hear what happened yesterday on Red Square?"

"Sandler told me."

"I intend to write a report about it and present it today at the editorial offices of *Pravda*."

Krasny's face lit up with surprise and delight. "How wonderful! But I can't believe they'll print it."

"Of course not. But I'll take it quickly from office to office. After that, I'll circulate it in manuscript."

"That's marvellous, Daniil! But what about Anna?"

"She wants me to do it."

THE EYEWITNESS REPORT

"Wonderful! Do you realize what a report like that from you may accomplish? It may prevent the authorities from bringing that brave group to trial."

"I'm hoping it will turn out that way. But if they *are* brought to trial, I'm ready to appear as a witness for the defence."

Krasny flung an arm around Barkov's shoulders and gave him a hug. "Now it's time to tell you why I came here. It wasn't just to let you know about myself. Julius tried to get me to inform on the other members of the Human Rights Committee. He thought he was being clever by beginning with open members like Sakharov, Grigorenko and Chalidze.* But then he read off a long list of other names. Some of them were secret members of the Committee, and some were not. To my surprise, your name was on the list."

"Guilt by association," Barkov said lightly. "We're friends, we see each other... a natural conclusion for the police."

"They'll feel positive of it when you circulate your account of the demonstration."

"That's not the only thing I intend to circulate," Barkov told him strongly. "I'm going to follow it immediately with something else!" He felt deep pride at the look on Krasny's face. "I can't stand it any more.* We both offered our lives to defend socialism. We have as much moral right to say what socialism should be as the men in the Kremlin. But listen," he added hastily, "don't take that to mean that I'm trying to make a decision for *you*. I don't need a laboratory to continue my profession – you do. Not everyone can play the same role."

Krasny nodded. "That's been on my mind since yesterday. I appreciate your mentioning it. Now listen... whatever I decide... I don't think we should meet or call each other for a while. Let's see how things go."

"I agree. How is Veronika taking this?"

"She's a fighter. She wants me to stand my ground. But I'm torn. I'm trying to conceive of life without work in a laboratory. It's very difficult. Then, again, maybe Julius was only sent to

CHAPTER 5

try and frighten me." He stood up. "Well... time to go. See if there's anyone outside the apartment, will you? That son of a bitch told me it would be held against me if I repeated what he had said."

The corridor outside the apartment was clear. Their eyes met in a final exchange as Krasny walked out. They had been warm friends for thirty-five years. Barkov closed the door and leant his head back against the wall. Softly he began to curse. It was happening again – the bureaucrats shitting on the people, insisting that only *their* ideas could be heard, only *their* tastes could be suffered to exist. Karl Marx had described socialism as "the Kingdom of Freedom".* It was a dream that never had become real before this year. For a few exciting months it had come to flower in Czechoslovakia – but then the Kremlin had crushed it. Yet a time would come when it would flower again.

How far away his novel seemed now! How unimportant his yearning to finish it at all costs, so that he could climb higher on the ladder of literary distinction! Yesterday at Execution Ground an invisible bugler had sounded a call to arms. He felt as he had twenty-six years before when he had embraced Anna, kissed her passionately and said goodbye. Both knew they might never meet again, but a train was waiting to take him and others to an army training camp. He had yearned never to be separated from her, but there was a greater urgency, and he had boarded the train.

So now... another train!

2

He sat down at his desk, picked up his ballpoint pen and wrote at the top of a sheet of the yellow paper he used for first drafts:

Eyewitness Report
by
Daniil Barkov

The beginning pages of almost anything he wrote usually went slowly and had to be revised more than once before he found the tone and rhythm he wanted. On this morning it was different: he felt at once that he was striking the right keys. He wrote rapidly, crossed out only occasionally, and had little need to pause in order to frame his next sentence. In less than an hour he had over five pages. His concentration was so intense that a knocking on his door went on for almost half a minute before he heard it. His desk was in the living room near the window. In the time that it took him to stride the length of the room, the knocking became more forceful, sounding as though two fists were belabouring the door. His first thought – that Ilya had returned – was discarded. Ilya wouldn't knock like that. He opened the door on five men he never had seen before, three of whom were carrying briefcases. One of them smiled pleasantly and asked if he was the author Daniil Petrovich Barkov.

"Yes."

The man held out an identification card and a legal paper with a seal on it. "I am Captain Yakunin, Criminal Investigation Division of the Public Prosecutor's Office. These two men are my subordinates. The two young ones there are citizen witnesses required by law."

A wave of heat surged through Barkov's body. Although he already knew the answer, he asked slowly, "Required by law for what?"

"We have instructions to search your apartment. Here is the warrant."

Barkov stared at him without raising his hand for the extended paper.

"Please look at it," the captain asked politely.

"The purpose of the search... what is it for?"

"In my position one is not at liberty to discuss instructions." His tone and manner became almost deferential. "I've admired your work for years, Comrade Barkov, so believe me when I say that this assignment was not welcome."

CHAPTER 5

Barkov's voice rose. "I will not let you come into my apartment until I have called the Prosecutor's Office and verified the warrant."

"Please do call the office, but I must ask you to leave the door open. We'll remain outside."

Barkov could find no valid reason for rejecting the compromise. He took the warrant with the realization that he was trembling from both indignation and a nameless fear. His brain raced as he walked slowly towards the telephone near his desk. What could it mean? Even if he had been photographed at the demonstration, he had been there only as a spectator. Why would that lead to a search of his apartment by the CID? Was there any possibility that it was connected to Julius's visit to Ilya? Unlikely! He was not even a secret member of the Human Rights Committee. In fact, since the time the Committee was formed, he had spent most of the year at Peredelkino.

He asked Information for the number of the Public Prosecutor's Office and quickly dialled it. The name signed to the warrant was that of Senior Investigator L.S. Shilova. When the switchboard answered, he gave his name and asked to speak to Comrade Shilova. He was put through to her so quickly that he was surprised.

"Ah, Comrade Barkov," a pleasant, cultivated voice said, "I'm glad you called. In fact, I apologize for not having called you first – I meant to, but something urgent interfered. Believe me, I regret that I had to order this routine search of your apartment."

"But what's the reason for it?"

"A charge has been made that you have been violating Article 190 of the Criminal Code."

Although he was familiar with the text of the article, Barkov was so shocked that he replied slowly, "Kindly tell me the specific section of the article with which I have been charged."

The cultivated voice replied lightly, as though it hardly mattered, "Section One... the dissemination by word of mouth, or in written form, of deliberate fabrications discrediting the Soviet political and social system."*

"That's absolute nonsense! Who made such a charge?"

"I also am positive it's nonsense," Investigator Shilova said apologetically, "but since it has been made, wouldn't you like to have it cleared up as soon as possible?"

"Of course! But who made it? Why is the *first* step a search of my apartment? Why didn't you call me in to confront the liar?"

The voice continued to be apologetic. "Comrade Barkov, although I'm a senior investigator, I am not at liberty to violate normal procedures. Things must be done in an orderly fashion. A search of your apartment is a necessary first step. I'm assuming that nothing will be found that would support the charge?"

"Of course not – ridiculous!"

"Then why object to it? A nuisance, but a required formality. By the way, if the investigators decide to remove anything for inspection, a precise inventory must be made. If they don't do this, or do it carelessly, I would like you to telephone me at once."

Barkov remained silent. He felt as though he were in a chess game with an opponent who was making pawn moves that seemed unimportant, yet were hemming him in.

"After the search is completed," Shilova continued, "I would like a brief chat with you. It will be your opportunity to refute the charge. Will you be willing to go along voluntarily with the investigators? You needn't come if you don't want to."

The pieces didn't fit, Barkov thought. If the conversation with Shilova was to be voluntary, why had a warrant been issued for a compulsory search? Yet it was obvious that an arrest warrant could also have been issued.

"Yes, I'll be glad to go with them. However, my wife is in the hospital and she expects me at four in the afternoon."

"There will be no problem about your visiting her, Comrade Barkov. By the way, did the investigators bring two citizen witnesses?"

CHAPTER 5

"Yes."

"Good. Sometimes they are lax about it. Until later then. Goodbye."

"Goodbye."

He was very disturbed. Everyone was polite, everyone was regretful, but he had been charged under 190/1, and an investigation was under way. He heard a cough and turned around. Captain Yakunin was no longer outside the apartment. He had stepped into the small entry from which he could observe Barkov. But naturally... he wouldn't want any papers destroyed.

"Come in," Barkov said, and felt foolish the moment the words slipped out. He was preserving a proprietorship he already had lost.

3

"Ah, a very attractive apartment," Captain Yakunin said amiably as he looked around. He was a few years younger than Barkov, about the same height, but a good fifteen kilos heavier. There was an expression of smiling contentment on his round, plump face. "Where would you like the witnesses to sit, Comrade Barkov?"

"Anywhere."

Yakunin gestured towards the couch, and the two sat down. One was a hulking blond youth of twenty who looked to be on the stupid side, the other had a book under his arm and might have been a university student. Barkov guessed that both were volunteers, auxiliary policemen rather than citizen witnesses casually encountered. If so, they should have been wearing identifying armbands, but he didn't care to make an issue of it. Yakunin next asked where one of his associates could sit if it became necessary to write any notes. Barkov gestured towards the desk, and Number Two strode towards it. He was in his early thirties, a short man with an overly serious, stern look, as though he were carrying the fate of Soviet society on his shoulders. The third investigator, smoking a pipe, began at once to study the books that occupied the entire length of one wall from floor to ceiling. He was in his late twenties – a handsome, athletic-looking man. Barkov realized with a sudden chill that all three of the CID men were neatly dressed in summer sport clothes of the same type and quality as the clothes worn by the KGB agents the day before. There was no logical reason for this to bother him, but it did.

Pointing to the wall opposite the bookshelves, Yakunin asked with a smile, "Is that Polish?" It was, in fact, a gift from Shika: a black paper cut-out mounted on a white mat, a charming example of folk art.

"Yes. How did you know?"

"I was in Poland with Army Intelligence for several years in the late Forties. I brought back half a dozen of them. Very decorative, aren't they?"

"Yes."

With the same beaming smile Yakunin asked, "Are both of those typewriters?" He was pointing to two cases on the floor by the desk.

Barkov nodded.

"Both belong to you?"

"One is mine, one is my wife's."

Yakunin's voice became crisp as he addressed Number Two. "Start your inventory with two typewriters. Open the cases. Mark down the brand name and the serial numbers."

"What is the reason for taking typewriters, captain?"

"Instructions, comrade." The polite manner had not disappeared, but a marked firmness had come into his tone. He sauntered over to the desk. Above it was a framed photograph of Solzhenitsyn. Barkov had cut it from a magazine six years before, when Solzhenitsyn's first novel had been published – the only one of his books allowed publication. "Ah!" Yakunin exclaimed. He opened his briefcase and

CHAPTER 5

put the photograph inside it. "Inventory! A photograph of Alexander Solzhenitsyn." He bent over the desk, stared at the two teeth on the saucer and turned to Barkov. "These look like teeth."

Barkov nodded, thinking hard. He already had written about the teeth in the pages of his *Report* lying on the desk. Almost certainly the captain would be reading them.

"They're associated with a report I'm writing for *Pravda*. I was in the middle of it when you knocked. It's there on my desk."

Yakunin picked up the 'Eyewitness Report'. He read the first two pages rapidly, began the third page and abruptly said, "Inventory! Five handwritten pages entitled 'Eyewitness Report'. He smiled blandly at Barkov. "I take it these two teeth fell from the mouth of the demonstrator?"

"Yes."

"And you picked them up?"

"Yes."

"Inventory: two teeth." He picked up Shika's letter, glanced at it and said, "Inventory: letter mailed from Warsaw dated twelve August."

"Does a search warrant give you the right to take private correspondence?"

"In the face of a search warrant, Comrade Barkov, nothing is exempt! I'm sorry, but you've been a soldier, so you know that orders, however unpleasant, must be followed."

Barkov warned himself sharply not to let his indignation get in the way of cool thinking. He had a serious need to appraise what was going on. However, as the search continued, he found it impossible to make an appraisal. It became clear at once that they wanted every self-published manuscript in his library. There weren't too many, since most of those he had were in his country home. However, they did find the first two issues of *A Chronicle of Current Events*, as well as the manuscripts of Solzhenitsyn's *First Circle** and

Sakharov's *Progress, Coexistence and Intellectual Freedom.**
But to what end? There was no law against reading uncensored books in manuscript form. Certainly sheer possession of the manuscripts could not be evidence against him under Article 190/1.

Yakunin opened a desk drawer and took out another manuscript. "Look here," Barkov said sharply, "that belongs to the Institute of World Economy and International Relations. It's a translation done by my wife."

"Nothing will be lost, comrade. What language was the original book in?" He opened a notebook.

"English."

"Published where, please?"

"In the United States."

"Written by whom?"

"By many authors, not one. It's called *The Soviet Union: The Fifty Years.** The contributors are reporters for the *New York Times*."

"Ah, the *New York Times*," Yakunin said, writing busily. "Nothing will be lost, comrade."

From another drawer Yakunin took a few pages of the chapter Barkov was working on. He recalled with relief that he had not given it a chapter number, but merely had entitled it "The Central Committee Member". Moreover, he had not yet reached the point in the chapter that would make the censors sit up and blink. He could say that it was a short story, and they wouldn't go hunting in his country home for the rest of the manuscript. Or – dismaying thought – were they already there?

There wasn't much correspondence in the apartment – most of it was in Peredelkino – but they took whatever they found.

"That painting," said Yakunin, pointing to a non-objective oil on the wall. "Who is the artist?"

"Vanya Nasedkin."

"Is he a member of the Artists' Union?"

CHAPTER 5

"I don't know. (He did know. Nasedkin had been expelled from the Artists' Union for rejecting the theory of socialist realism as a guide to painting.)

"And that?" Yakunin was pointing to the reproduction of a cubist work that Barkov had bought in Budapest.

"The artist is Picasso."*

"Inventory! One oil painting by Nasedkin. One print by Picasso."

When they moved into the kitchen, Barkov followed them, but there was nothing of interest to them there. However, there was a moment of personal interchange when he drank a glass of tap-water. Number Three asked with surprise, "How is it you don't boil your water, comrade? It's dangerous not to." Barkov explained that in the Kutuzovsky district the water mains were new, and there was no danger of contamination through seepage. Number Three nodded with interest, and Yakunin led the way into the bedroom, where business took over again. Number Three dragged a box from under the bed and took out two albums of personal photographs. Yakunin, opening the drawers of a wardrobe, found it relevant to his mission to inventory Barkov's Medal of Honour as well as the decorations he had received for his Stalin and Lenin prizes. Rubbing his palms together, he then said politely, "If you are ready, Comrade Barkov, I think we can take you to see Comrade Shilova now. That is, of course, if you are willing."

"I'm quite willing."

"May I use your telephone?"

Barkov nodded. By this time he had become annoyed with the deferential tone Yakunin was employing. It was obvious that it was hypocritical. However, when he heard him say, "This is Captain Yakunin. Please tell Comrade Shilova we're leaving now," he felt a little better about things. Shilova had been too friendly also, but with her he would be able to get to the bottom of this bizarre business.

4

There was a large Volga in front of his apartment house with thick, grey curtains on its back and side windows. The two citizen witnesses, who had not said a word in the apartment, now strolled off down the street without being dismissed by Yakunin. It appeared clear that they had been instructed beforehand to do this. Number Two got in the front to drive. Number Three and the captain flanked Barkov in the rear.

The moment the auto started, Number Three, who had said very little in the apartment, began to chatter in a lively manner. He owned all of Barkov's books, and regretted that he had not known he was going to meet him. If he had, he would have brought them along and asked for his autograph.

Something indefinable in the tone and manner of this handsome, pipe-smoking athlete made Barkov wonder whether he ever had read a word he had written. With his eyes on the man's face he said, "I would have been glad to autograph them for you. Tell me, which one do you like best?"

The chattering mouth was suddenly at a loss for words.

"Was it *The Living and the Dead*? I hope so, because it's my favourite."

"Mine also – that's the one."

It was not important to Barkov to tell him *The Living and the Dead* had been written by Konstantin Simonov.* Of more importance was the reason why a CID officer had been instructed to play this game with him. He turned to look at Yakunin, and was greeted by the amiable smile that was as fixed on his face as though painted on a doll.

Where are we? Barkov wondered suddenly. The combination of the side curtains and the chatter of Number Three had distracted him from following the route they were taking. Looking through the front window, he saw with surprise that they were on an avenue not immediately recognizable, certainly nowhere near Pushkin Street or even the centre of Moscow.

CHAPTER 5

"We're not going to the Public Prosecutor's Building," he said to the captain. "Where are you taking me?"

"Comrade Shilova didn't want you recognized. Too many people come and go at the main office. She decided to interview you at a local precinct, so that she could keep it informal."

Did the pieces fit? They did and they didn't. He felt confused. Confused, uneasy and anxious. These were not the Stalin days, when people were arbitrarily arrested and shot out of hand. He was not afraid of that. Nevertheless...

The auto turned into an unfamiliar street. Almost at once it swung into a driveway. Barkov could see several ambulances, a ramp leading up to closed doors and a sign above them that said "Emergency Entrance". He turned to Yakunin with astonishment as the car stopped. "This is a hospital. What are we doing here?"

The reply was soft, accompanied by the painted smile. "Before Investigator Shilova has her talk with you she wants to have a clear picture of your state of health."

"*What?* That's ridiculous! I'm leaving you."

The captain's hands, which had been on his lap beneath his briefcase, moved quickly and deftly. One link of a pair of handcuffs snapped around Barkov's left wrist. A second later he closed the other link on his own right wrist.

Stunned, Barkov stared at the cold metal clamping his wrist. Then he erupted with a violent shout. "By what right? Do you have a warrant? I demand to see a warrant for my arrest!"

Yakunin thrust a red identity card in front of Barkov's eyes. "Do you recognize it?" There was no amiability in his voice now.

The letters KGB were prominent on the card.

"We were ordered to bring you here for an examination. There is no warrant, because, for your own good, there is to be no public knowledge of this private event. Now come with me!"

Yakunin turned, opened the door and started to move out of the auto, but Barkov pulled his left arm back hard, swinging

Yakunin's body around. "No public knowledge?" he shouted wildly. "I'll make it so public the whole country will know about it!"

Barkov's right arm was suddenly and painfully twisted behind his back by Number Two. With neat coordination he was both pushed and pulled out of the car, where he stumbled to one knee on the pavement. He was yanked to his feet and rapidly moved up the ramp. He felt wild rage, powerful fears and, above all, bewilderment to the point of believing that none of this was happening, that somehow he would awaken to find it had been a nightmare.

The double hospital doors were opened by unseen hands. He was thrust into a corridor, where two tall, powerfully built men wearing hospital gowns confronted him. One moved behind him and shut the doors. Yakunin unlocked the handcuff. Smiling, he said, "My apologies, comrade. When I am given orders, I have no choice."

One orderly partially opened one of the hospital doors, but kept his eyes on Barkov while doing so. There was no chance to break free. Yakunin and Number Two slipped out. The door was closed and locked with a key on a ring, and then the ring went into the orderly's trouser pocket beneath the white coat. The orderly in front smiled in a friendly way, showing big, steel-capped teeth. His face, despite the smile, looked hard and cold. Yet, when he spoke, it was in a bland, matter-of-fact way. "I'm Grigory. He's Kolya. Walk straight ahead, please."

"Are you also from the Security Police?" Barkov asked. His voice was hoarse from tension.

"Oh no, just hospital orderlies."

"If the KGB wants to know my state of health, it can always get my medical records from my polyclinic. Why was I brought here?"

"I imagine a different type of diagnosis is needed," the bland voice replied. "This is a psychiatric hospital."

"*What?*" It was almost a scream.

CHAPTER 5

"For that reason all windows are barred, all doors are locked. Patients who do not behave themselves are forcibly restrained." He pointed down the long, empty corridor. "This way, Daniil Petrovich."

There was a pause while Barkov fought to control his volcanic feelings. They knew his name... they had been expecting him. Shilova had signed the search warrant, but from the beginning it had been an operation of the Security Police. For what purpose?

Slowly he walked down the corridor. Grigory was at his side, Kolya two metres behind. Barkov's rage was so enormous that for the moment he felt no fear.

Chapter 6

I

Fear came soon enough, however. They walked to the end of the corridor, where Grigory unlocked a door. They entered a good-sized room in which the windows, backed by steel bars, were shut. It was stiflingly hot. Grigory locked the door. On one side of the room there were shelves with wire baskets containing clothes. On the other side there were two shower baths. Grigory told him to remove everything from his pockets – and then to turn all of his pockets inside out. Kolya, who was a genial-looking, blue-eyed giant of about thirty, took his billfold, wristwatch and keys. He wrote out a receipt. He then inventoried each article of clothing while dropping them into a wire basket.

It was only when Barkov was naked that he felt fear in his belly, as he had so often during the war. Two men had directed him to remove his clothes, and he had obeyed them – he, Daniil Barkov, had obeyed because he was physically unable to resist. He, Barkov, had been forcibly locked up in a mental institution.

"Open your mouth and stick out your tongue," said Grigory. He examined Barkov's mouth with the aid of a pencil flashlight. "Bend over and pull your buttocks apart." The flashlight was directed at Barkov's rectum. "Now take a shower." Kolya handed him a towel.

"I showered two hours ago."

"All new patients shower! Soap yourself well."

He showered and dried his body. He put on the striped pyjamas, the grey robe, the fibre slippers handed him by Kolya. His mind was impaled by a single spike: why? He had violated no law. He had not been formally arrested. Yakunin had even made a comic remark: that it was for his own good. But he also could hear that smug voice saying something bizarre and possibly sinister: "There is to be no public knowledge of this private event." What event? Private to what end? He knew of a number of cases in which outspoken political dissenters like General Grigorenko had been arrested, subjected to a psychiatric examination – however specious – declared mentally incompetent after a formal court hearing, and then confined in an institution. But *he* had *not* been arrested. And he had done nothing of a public nature to place himself in the ranks of the dissenters or to attract the attention of the KGB.

None of the pieces fit! *When* had the decision been made to incarcerate him? Why today and not yesterday or last week? The KGB had not ordered an arrest, yet they had worked out an elaborate strategy of deception that involved a search of his apartment, their own agents pretending to be CID investigators from the Public Prosecutor's Office, a false appointment with Shilova, lies, excuses and a kidnapping. For what purpose?

Kolya handed him a carbon copy of the receipt for his valuables and another for the inventory of his clothing.

"This way," said Grigory.

2

They returned to the empty corridor. They turned a corner and walked a few metres to another unmarked door. Grigory unlocked it. They entered, and the door was locked again. The small room had no windows, and was an oven. There were a few chairs, a small end table with newspapers and magazines on it, and ceiling lights behind frosted glass. Grigory turned a chair around so that it faced the wall. "You will please sit down with your hands on your head."

Barkov obeyed, remembering as he did so a scene from Solzhenitsyn's *First Circle*, in which a high-ranking member of the Ministry of Foreign Affairs was arrested. He recalled the

CHAPTER 6

seismic shock the man had felt. It was the same with him... only the word earthquake could describe his feelings.

"If you move your hands from your head, it will be a sign to Kolya that you intend to attack him."

Grigory walked across the room and opened another door. As soon as he left, Kolya stepped up behind Barkov and began whispering to him. "Do please keep your hands on your head, but don't let that bastard frighten you. He likes to feel he's a big shot. I must say it's an honour to meet you, Daniil Petrovich, although naturally I wish the circumstances were different. I don't know why you're here, but it doesn't seem to me you have anything to worry about. You don't act loony, not one bit. Anyway, the doctors here are smart. They know how to separate the sheep from the goats... Well, now, I better stop talking." He stepped away.

Friend or foe? Barkov wondered. He didn't know.

A door creaked slightly, and Grigory returned. "Get up, please. Come with me."

Kolya winked as Barkov passed by him.

Two doors, another corridor, and they entered what seemed to be a medical examining room. Several windows with bars behind them were open and looked out on an empty courtyard. The temperature was comfortable. Behind a desk, wearing the medal of a Hero of Labour on her white coat, was a grey-haired woman in her sixties with intelligent, sad eyes and a tired face. Grigory said to her, "I'll be in the corridor. If the patient is not cooperative, call me." To Barkov he said, "At the other end of the examining rooms there is a locked door. The doctor doesn't have a key to it."

He went out.

"I am Doctor Lyubinskaya," the woman said softly. "Sit down please." She waited until he had done so and then continued. "I have your medical charts from your polyclinic. I would like to look them over before I begin my examination. I'm a neurologist."

As the doctor opened the folder, Barkov chewed on what she had told him. The fact that the KGB had commandeered his medical charts was further proof of the planning involved. Presumably the purpose of a neurological examination was to find some physiological reason to justify his incarceration. But if they actually wanted to declare him insane, why hadn't they arrested him? "There is to be no public knowledge of this private event." Once again the pieces didn't fit.

His attention was caught by the fact that Doctor Lyubinskaya was writing rapidly on a pad. When she finished, she did something odd. She picked up a scissor, cut what she had written away from the rest of the sheet and then held the strip in front of her so that he could read it – yet so close to the desk that she could turn it face down in an instant. He leant forward tensely.

> Esteemed Daniil Petrovich: silence – microphones in these rooms! I don't know why you've been brought here, but I know it was by order of the KGB. When you are examined by the psychiatrists, behave calmly. Give them no grounds to find abnormalities of thought or conduct.

Barkov gave her a slight nod and a tight smile of appreciation. The doctor quickly cut the strip into three parts, rolled them into separate pellets and put them into her mouth. She picked up a glass of water and swallowed them. Then she bent over his medical records again.

Barkov's pulse was racing uncomfortably fast. He felt trust in this woman, and he was shaken by her warning. Suddenly the pieces did fit. Even though he had not been formally arrested, *that* was no longer the important factor. Depending upon the will of the Security Police, he could be arrested *after* incarceration as well as before. Since there were no grounds for him to be examined by psychiatrists, his kidnapping had been the first step of an entrapment. And even though he didn't know why, it now was shockingly clear that his sanity was going to

CHAPTER 6

be tested. If by honest psychiatrists, he had no worry. But what if they were dishonest – pawns of the KGB?

He remembered something appalling. The first issue of *A Chronicle of Current Events*, which had started circulating hand to hand at the end of April, had reprinted an appeal signed by half a dozen civil-rights activists. They had sent their appeal to a conference of world Communist parties in Budapest. In addition to protesting the prosecution of various Soviet citizens who held unorthodox political convictions, they specifically mentioned the illegal, forcible confinement of healthy individuals in mental hospitals. At the time he had assumed this to be a reference to the several cases he had known about in the past – the mathematician Yesenin-Volpin,* the geophysicist Samsonov* and General Grigorenko – each of them now at liberty. But what if there were others he had not heard about? How did he know the practice was not more widespread than he realized? When press, radio, television, the police, the courts, were all controlled by the government, many things could happen that the public never became aware of.

Ah, but there was no need to lose balance or become panicky. Daniil Barkov simply couldn't vanish without notice. Anna was expecting him at four. Shilova had said there would be no problem about his meeting that appointment. If she had lied, Anna would not be indifferent to his failure to appear or to get in touch with her. There would be calls to the apartment, to friends, to the Writers' Union, the Cinema Club – and finally to the police. And Lidia would be waiting for him in the lobby of the Ukraina at seven. Lidia would not be lethargic about it either.

No, for the moment he would accept that Shilova had not lied. By his guess it still was not noon. There was no reason he might not be out of this damned place before four o'clock. In any instance, he absolutely would follow the doctor's advice when the psychiatrists interviewed him. He would behave calmly, and he would scrutinize their questions for hidden traps.

Doctor Lyubinskaya said, "I congratulate you. You seem to be in excellent health. I judge that your war wounds have not troubled you in these years?"

"No, doctor." He wondered what her story was, and why her eyes were so sad.

"Are your parents living?"

"No."

The doctor began to take notes. "How old were they when they died, and what was the cause of death?"

"My father had a stroke when he was fifty-six. It was two days after the Nazi invasion, and I've always believed there was a connection."

"It's possible, but we never know," the doctor murmured. "What about your mother?"

"She died in a traffic accident. That was during the war also. She was forty-three."

"Was the accident your mother's fault?"

"No. She was waiting in line for a bus. A truck skidded and ran up on the sidewalk."

"Did either of your parents have any mental disorders?"

"No."

"Epileptic seizures?"

"No."

"Was either of them a heavy drinker?"

"No."

"Did they ever speak of any mental illness in a relative?"

"No."

"Do you have brothers or sisters?"

"I had a younger brother. He was killed at the front in '45."

Doctor Lyubinskaya looked at him in silence for a moment, and he suddenly felt sure he knew her story: that she was one of the many women who had lost her husband and all her sons in the war. He felt such compassion for her he wanted to reach out and touch her hand, but he did not.

"Do you smoke?"

CHAPTER 6

"No."

"Have you ever spent a night in a sobering-up station?"

"No."

"Do you suffer from insomnia?"

"No."

The questions continued, and so did his negative replies. Dizziness? Convulsions? Hallucinations? Temporary deafness? A ringing or whistling in his ears?

"Have you ever beaten your wife?"

The question caught him unawares, and he replied indignantly, "I should say not!"

The doctor smiled, and the questions were resumed: double vision? Difficulty in swallowing? A sensation of pricking, tingling or creeping on his skin? Any loss of rectal control?

The verbal examination ended after about five minutes, and the doctor asked him to walk to the door and return. She made a note, and then began a number of tests he was familiar with from his yearly physical at the polyclinic. She asked him to close his eyes, extend his hands and touch the tip of his nose with the forefinger of one hand, then the other. She had him extend his hands again, this time with the palms up. With her own forefinger she wrote a number on the palm of his left hand and asked him what it was.

"Two."

She murmured "Good" and wrote on his right palm.

"Five."

She told him to open his eyes, grip her right hand and squeeze it. He did so with an appreciative smile, and she responded with a quick smile of her own. After that, she tested his reflexes – tapping his knees, ankles, elbows with a rubber hammer. He knew from her glance that it was not an accident when she muttered "Good". She told him to lie down. She held a tuning fork to each ankle and asked him to tell her when the vibration stopped. After that, she tested his sense of touch with a wisp of cotton flicking his thighs, belly and chest, and his response to pain with light pin pricks. Once again she murmured "Good" for the benefit of the microphones. The examination ended finally with her giving him an electroencephalogram that lasted a tedious half-hour. She made some notes and then said, "I congratulate you again. Your neurological responses are completely normal." She pressed a buzzer on her desk.

He looked at her appreciatively, and his lips silently spoke the word "Thanks". She nodded, and her sad eyes regarded him with compassion. Then she looked down at her notes. A few moments later Kolya came in.

3

When they were back in the long, empty corridor, Kolya said with his genial smile, "I've got news. Your psychiatric interview is scheduled for one thirty. I imagine you'll be walking out of here an hour or two later."

Barkov kept the edge out of his voice. "Why do you think so? You know I was brought here by force – you saw the handcuffs."

"That's right, and I'd like to know why. Patients come in here in one of two ways: after an arrest, if they've done something nutty, or by the decision of a psychiatrist or an ordinary doctor. But since you didn't, it's got me wondering. If you don't mind, have you been up to anything? I mean, like screwing the wife of some top Party leader?"

"No."

"Any other reason you can think of?"

"No."

"Well, whatever's behind this, it can't lead to anything serious. As I told you earlier, the doctors here are sharp as razors. They'll know right off you're not loony."

It sounded comforting, but for some reason Kolya didn't inspire the trust that Doctor Lyubinskaya had. Barkov wondered why, and couldn't find an explanation.

CHAPTER 6

At the end of the corridor Kolya unlocked a door that opened on a small courtyard in which there was a volleyball net. As they crossed to another door, he asked if Barkov ever had visited a psychiatric hospital.

"No."

"As a writer I imagine you'll be interested. Of course, we're only going to a quiet ward – the violent loony bins are more dramatic." He unlocked a door, and they stepped into another long, empty corridor. Kolya stopped at the first door and pressed a bell button. After a moment, they were admitted by another orderly, who, like Kolya and Grigory, was in his early thirties, over six feet tall and powerfully built.

The sound of balalaika music in the ward made a pleasant first impression. About thirty men in striped pyjamas were lying or sitting on cots, which were so close together that only the narrowest of aisles separated them. A few men were pacing back and forth in a small open area, in which there was a table with newspapers and magazines. Even though two barred windows along one wall were open, the room was hot. Above the windows there was a framed lithograph. With his hand outstretched, Lenin was surveying the patients with a benign smile.

Kolya gestured for Barkov to sit at the newspaper table and took a chair beside him. "The midday meal has been served already, but one of the orderlies is going to bring us something." He lowered his voice. "If any of the psychos speak to you, don't tell them your surname."

"Can you tell me what time it is?"

"One o'clock."

A half-hour in which to stew in the juices of his indignation and anxiety! He decided to make conversation. "That man plays the balalaika very well. Why is he in here?"

"He's a music teacher, but he turns into a devil when he drinks heavy. Beats his wife, his children, even his mother. He's been an outpatient for years, but this time he went too far – broke his wife's wrist and fractured her skull. I hate a man who abuses women. If it was up to me, I'd ship him to a psychiatric colony."

"I never heard of psychiatric colonies."

"They're for loonies who are socially dangerous and incurable. You never heard of them because no one who goes in ever comes out. Did you ever hear of a special psychiatric hospital?"

"Is it different from the one we're in?"

"Different?" Kolya chuckled sourly. "It's called a hospital, but actually it's a prison. The cells are called wards. I worked in one for two days and quit. Nobody gets cured there – they just get dosed with drugs. What a madhouse! I was afraid I'd go psycho myself!"

"But you don't mind being here?"

"Oh, no. Here the patients get diagnosed and get treatment. After a couple of weeks they either become outpatients or else they're shipped to some other place. Now, you take that psycho over there. The last bed in the last row. They put him there because he's so disgusting."

The patient he indicated was a young, fair-haired man sitting cross-legged on his cot. His pyjama top was open, and he was picking at his chest with his forefinger.

"He's got sores all over his body," Kolya said with distaste. "The doctors don't know what they come from, but he keeps picking at them until they bleed. As if that wasn't bad enough, he jerks off in front of everybody." Kolya shook his head. "But he's not socially dangerous, you see, he only harms himself. So he'll be sent to a mental hospital for chronic patients. Maybe the doctors there will cure him."

"By the way, what's the name of this hospital?"

"It's a district psychiatric hospital," Kolya replied. "Well, we're getting some food at last."

I am not supposed to know the name of the hospital, Barkov reflected. No, Kolya was no friend. He was playing a role as Shilova had played hers. And the talk about psychiatric colonies

CHAPTER 6

and special hospitals had not been casual conversation. There had been a purpose to that also.

An orderly with a tray came up to them. Their meal consisted of a large piece of salt herring, bread, boiled potatoes, tea with two lumps of sugar and a gesture at a fruit compote that Kolya, laughing, called "compote schizoid". The latter consisted of a small glass of water containing a slice of canned peach, three raisins and a single cooked cherry. Kolya attacked the meal with relish, but Barkov had little appetite and only picked at his food. He was very disturbed – eager for the psychiatric interview, but fearful of it. Kolya had said that patients were brought to this hospital in one of two ways: after an arrest if they had done something that appeared to be abnormal, or by the decision of a doctor or a psychiatrist. Did that mean that an hour from now a psychiatrist obedient to the Security Police might formally order his commitment?

"I'd like to ask a question. Let's say a psychiatrist orders a patient brought to his hospital. A psychiatrist can make a mistake like any other person. Does that mean—"

"I can answer you," Kolya interrupted. "One psychiatrist can decide that a citizen needs to be examined in a hospital as an inpatient, whether he likes it or not. But only a commission of three psychiatrists can decide that a patient must *remain* in the hospital."

"Will I be seeing a commission, then?"

"I imagine. Aren't you going to eat your herring?"

"No. You're welcome to it if you want it."

Kolya did want it. Barkov drank his tea and ate a piece of bread. The information about a commission made him feel easier.

A short, stout youth of eighteen came up to Kolya. There was a timid, anxious look on his face. "Excuse me, are you a doctor?"

"No. An orderly. "

"Good! I don't trust the doctors here, not one of them." He held out his hand. "What do you see?"

"Your hand."

"And what's on my hand?"

"Nothing."

"You too?" the youth exclaimed despairingly. "Don't you see the bugs on my hand?"

"There are no bugs on your hand."

"I see them and I feel them. I brush them off, but they always come back. Yet nobody believes me." Close to tears he shook his head and wandered off.

Kolya laughed. "You can't imagine what we get in here. Yesterday we shipped out a loony who would lie all day on his cot laughing to himself. You see that big, curly-haired man over there with the mole on his cheek?"

"Yes."

"He's a degenerate – raped his six-year-old daughter. Oh, we get beauties in here all right. Sometimes I think about applying for the night shift. It's easier on the nerves – you have less to do with the patients. But with night work I'd miss the jazz programme on Voice of America. Do you listen to it?"

"No."

"I'm crazy about jazz, just loony for it."

"Do you mind telling me the time?"

"It's one twenty-two. We might as well get moving."

4

Kolya led him to a small waiting room on the second floor, where Grigory was smoking a cigarette and reading a sports magazine. Kolya left with a smile and a nod. Grigory locked the door and resumed reading without saying anything.

"Behave calmly," Doctor Lyubinskaya had written.

But it was incredible! He was Daniil Barkov, author, prizewinner, his work translated into a dozen foreign languages!

CHAPTER 6

Nevertheless, he was wearing striped pyjamas, a grey robe and fibre slippers, and the palms of his hands were moist... as Ilya's palm had been moist when they shook hands. Yet Ilya had only been threatened, not forcibly incarcerated.

"Behave calmly. Give them no grounds to find abnormalities of thought or conduct."

Chapter 7

I

A buzzer sounded softly. Grigory opened an unlocked door opposite Barkov and gestured for him to enter the adjacent room. Inside, seated behind a rectangular table, were a man and woman in white coats. The woman immediately stood up and came around to greet him. She was in her late thirties – a statuesque, handsome brunette. She smiled warmly as she extended her hand. "It's an honour to meet you, Daniil Petrovich. I'm Doctor Larina, Deputy Chief Psychiatrist."

Barkov nodded, forced a tiny, mechanical smile, briefly shook her hand.

"And this is Doctor Rubin."

The latter stood up. "A great pleasure." He extended his hand across the table. He was in his early thirties, slender, tall, with a serious, intelligent face, thick eyeglasses and – to Barkov's distress – the short haircut worn by soldiers in training. There was no logical reason for him to be made uneasy by a haircut, but he was.

"Please sit down," said Doctor Larina as she returned to the other side of the table.

Barkov cast a quick glance around. He saw that Grigory had left the room and closed the door. To his right there were two open windows with bars through which he could see a patch of grey sky. The room was warm, but not uncomfortable. The newly painted white walls were free of distracting decorations – even Lenin was missing.

"Would you care for some cold lemonade?" Doctor Larina asked. On the table there was a tray with a pitcher and four glasses.

"No thank you."

"Boris?"

Doctor Rubin shook his head, and she poured a glass for herself. Observing her, Barkov guessed that she had travelled abroad and that she moved in high circles. Her white coat was unbuttoned, and the quality and cut of what he could see of her purple dress spoke of a garment purchased in the West. So also did the lipstick, and the cameo pin and matching earrings.

"How do you feel, Daniil Petrovich?"

His mind repeated his first name and patronymic. Daniil, the son of Pyotr, who had been so proud to be an Old Bolshevik. How would his father have conducted himself in this situation? With discipline and shrewdness. With iron discipline!

He replied slowly in a controlled, quiet voice, "The only way a normal man could feel in my situation – indignant."

She smiled gently. "Of course, it's the usual reaction. An individual slides into abnormal behaviour without being aware of it. However, others notice – members of the family, friends or co-workers, and they report it – it's their human duty. But the individual himself feels outraged when he is asked to submit to an examination by psychiatrists."

Barkov felt a powerful urge both to laugh and to shout at her with fury, but he pressed his hands flat on his thighs and continued to speak calmly. "Tell me, doctor, who was it that reported my alleged abnormal behaviour?"

"I don't know. Our chief of Psychiatry, Doctor Kulagin, merely told us to give you a preliminary examination because of a report he had received. He also gave us some materials to study that were taken from your apartment this morning."

"I see. Is it usual to search the apartment of someone who is to receive a psychiatric examination?"

"It depends upon the case. In some instances a diary or letters may be very revealing. Or the condition of the apartment itself! Any number of things may be helpful in our evaluation."

CHAPTER 7

"Does it also help to have the patient kidnapped by deceit and force? To deprive someone of his liberty is a serious crime." He deliberately didn't add that both of them were participating in that crime.

Doctor Larina's long-lashed, hazel eyes regarded him with astonishment. "Kidnapped? What exactly do you mean?"

"Force?" exclaimed Doctor Rubin. "It was my understanding that you came here from your polyclinic at the suggestion of your physician."

Once again he was being presented with pieces of a puzzle that did not fit. Were they both accomplished liars or did they really not know how he had been brought here? "Doctor Rubin," he asked slowly, "if I had come here voluntarily, who is it that would have ordered a search of my apartment?"

"Your physician could have requested it of the Public Prosecutor's Office."

"I see. Shall I tell you the circumstances of my arrival here?"

"Please do," said Doctor Larina.

He watched them closely as he reported what had occurred from the time Captain Yakunin first knocked at his door. Both of them exchanged surprised glances.

"But that's unheard of – it's completely irregular," said Doctor Larina.

"In that case you will, of course, see that I am immediately discharged?"

"Neither of us has the authority to do that. It could only be the decision of the chief psychiatrist."

"Then please tell him what happened."

"He's not in the hospital at present, and he's not expected for several hours."

"Besides," Doctor Rubin added, "there's something I must point out to you in all candour. I hope you won't take offence. Patients are frequently brought here by force as the result of an arrest. When they arrive, they may be calm and appear normal. Yet only the day before they may have committed some act of utter insanity. At this moment Doctor Larina and I have no objective way of determining whether you are telling us the truth when you say you were kidnapped by Security Police. That in itself – please forgive me – is an extremely bizarre story."

The heat mounted in Barkov's body, and he gripped his thighs. "All you need do is telephone the Public Prosecutor's Office. Ask for Chief Investigator Shilova. I presume she'll confirm that no arrest warrant was signed."

"That's exactly the point. If no arrest warrant was issued, it's impossible to believe that the Security Police will admit to an *illegal* kidnapping."

"But I say I *was* kidnapped! Is it of no importance to you to find out if I'm telling the truth?"

"Dear Daniil Petrovich," Doctor Larina interposed gently, "please think of it this way: you have reason to feel baffled, but in whatever manner you *were* brought here, *we* were instructed by the chief psychiatrist to give you a preliminary examination. We have no choice but to do it."

"And what if I refuse to be examined?"

"You'll leave me no alternative – you'll be returned to the ward. But I hope you won't refuse. In your place I personally would welcome an examination, because I would know that the psychiatrists were my friends. We are trained to help people, not harm them."

"But what if I don't need psychiatric help?"

"Then that will become clear. Since you say that you have been falsely charged with abnormal behaviour, why don't you take for granted that after an examination we will agree with you and recommend your discharge? You then can protest formally to various authorities about the way in which you were mistreated. You are, after all, a citizen of distinction. A letter from you to the Central Committee will not be brushed aside. I presume also that you can enlist the assistance of the Writers' Union."

CHAPTER 7

As in the phone conversation with Shilova, Barkov had the uneasy feeling that he was in a chess game with someone who was making small pawn moves that somehow were hemming him in. It was outrageous for him to be subjected to a psychiatric examination, but still more demeaning to be kept in a locked ward. He decided to try a move of his own. "Look here, my wife is ill, she's in the Academy of Sciences Hospital and she expects me at four o'clock. If I don't arrive, there will be telephone calls that will start with my apartment and then radiate all over Moscow and to Peredelkino as well. There will be quite a scandal over this."

"Excuse me, but you are, so to speak, blowing up a balloon without reason. Our examination can be completed in time for you to see your wife at four o'clock."

Barkov looked intently at her handsome face, then at Doctor Rubin. He couldn't detect guile in the countenance of either of them. What to do? A remark of Kolya's flashed into his mind: that only a commission of three psychiatrists could decide whether or not a patient should remain in a hospital.

"You're saying then that after you have examined me you have the authority to order my release?"

"To recommend it to the chief psychiatrist."

"Can you order my detention?"

"No. That can only be done by a commission of three psychiatrists."

"And what about the Security Police, who brought me here in the first place?"

"Psychiatric decisions are made by psychiatrists. We don't consult any body of police, including the KGB."

"Unless, of course, they have a specific report to give us," Doctor Rubin interjected. "If a murder or some antisocial behaviour has been committed, we naturally can't ignore it. But the decision as to mental competence is ours alone."

Barkov hesitated, then said slowly, "In that case, please proceed with your examination."

Doctor Larina smiled warmly. "A sensible decision. Are you sure you wouldn't enjoy some lemonade?"

"Yes, I would like some."

Doctor Rubin poured glasses for both of them. He offered Barkov a cigarette. When the latter refused, he put the cardboard tip of one between his own lips, but didn't light it.

"Now then," said Doctor Larina, "have you been feeling your usual self of late?"

"Yes."

"Any problem sleeping?"

"No."

"Any worries?"

"Yes. Are you aware of my wife's state of health?"

"No."

He told them what her condition was.

"But of course," said Doctor Larina sympathetically, "you would have to be a stone not to be worried about her."

Why was it, Barkov asked himself, that he kept feeling she was deceiving him the same way Investigator Shilova had? The smile was warm, the manner candid: she had said nothing amiss – but he felt that ahead of him lay entrapment.

"Daniil Petrovich," said Doctor Rubin, "there's a curious coincidence in our meeting today. Only a week ago I was having a conversation about you with my nephew. He's entering his second year of secondary school, and he knew that one of his assignments would be a report on your *Letters to a Foreign Journalist*. He had seen the book on my shelves and asked to borrow it. He was deeply affected by it, and yet, at the same time, a trifle sceptical – typical of his generation. He wanted to know if you had exaggerated the extent of the destruction our country suffered during the Patriotic War,* or exaggerated the rapidity of reconstruction... and so on. It's been quite some years since I first read it, so I leafed over it in order to discuss it with him. I was impressed again with what a splendid work it is."

CHAPTER 7

"Thank you."

"May I ask how you came to write it?"

"I explained that in my preface."

"I didn't reread the preface. Would you tell me?"

Barkov didn't know what relevance the question had in a psychiatric examination, but he saw no dangers in it. In addition, since Shilova had said that he had been charged with fabrications discrediting the Soviet system, it seemed like a good opportunity to talk freely to the contrary. "In 1952 my wife was assigned to be the translator-guide to an American journalist who wanted to write a series of articles about our post-war reconstruction. Since I understand English, I accompanied them. We covered a good part of the territory the Hitlerites had occupied. It was a particularly revealing trip, because in every village and city massive destruction was still visible, but enormous reconstruction was going on. It so happened that we also visited territory I had moved through as a foot soldier. I remember showing him in one village the exact spot where we found a dozen hanged partisans. One of them was a girl of about seventeen, whose tortured face never left my mind from then on." Barkov paused for a moment, his brows knitting. "It's odd... one saw death so often in the war that I never can explain why the face of that one poor girl haunted me so much. Anyway, the point about this is that we found out quickly that the journalist was amazingly ignorant. He was intelligent, rather charming, but he didn't know what life had been like under the tsars, or how socialism had transformed our country. So my wife and I used the many hours we spent together to give him an education. He seemed keenly interested, and took down many pages of notes. We tried to be absolutely truthful – we were not interested in disguising our shortcomings. But, for instance, he didn't know that under the tsars the people had been seventy-five per cent illiterate, while now we had an immense system of free education with universities and scientific institutes where there never even had been a schoolroom.

He didn't know either that we had a system of free medical and hospital care that no capitalist country had – and so on. Well, about five months later, he sent us a dozen articles he had written. They were beyond belief. It was as though he hadn't spent a moment with us. For instance, like so many other foreign journalists, he made a big thing out of the fact that women did physical work in our country. He made no mention of our explanation – that when a nation had lost over thirty million men in two world wars and a civil war, it naturally must make use of the labour power of women to an unusual degree. And at the same time he carefully avoided mentioning the fact that our country had opened all professions to our women – that it had liberated them in a way no capitalist nation ever has. Well, the short of it was that I exploded with indignation. I decided to answer him with a short book that might reach the people who had read his articles."

"Did it?"

"No. Those were the severest years of the Cold War. In Italy and France my book had considerable circulation, because of the size of the Communist parties there, but in the United States and most Western countries it didn't reach many readers."

"Nevertheless," Doctor Rubin observed admiringly, "year after year it accomplishes an important educational task for *our* youth. I realized the other day that it was not merely the dramatic manner in which you presented your facts that made the book so impressive, it's also the passion with which it was written. One knows that the author loves his country. You are eloquent in describing the terrible trials of the war, but you are even more eloquent in describing our marvellous accomplishments. One feels the enormous vitality of the socialist system in your book."

"Thank you. I'm delighted you feel that way."

"Tell me, if you were asked now to prepare a revised edition of it, what changes would you make? After all, sixteen years have passed."

CHAPTER 7

Barkov again heard Shilova's voice saying, "Article 190 of the Criminal Code." His antenna told him that Rubin must be probing in that direction.

"Naturally, some things would remain the same. For instance, the fact that education and health care are universal and free. However, our great successes in our space programme, in missile technology and in the enormous construction of prefabricated apartment houses had not yet begun. And when I wrote the book we were not yet the second industrial power of the world." He paused for a moment and added deliberately, "Of course, it would be necessary to deal with the terrible abuse of power under Stalin which we didn't know about in 1952, the violations of socialist legality and so on. Unless that were done, students would reject the book as a whole."

"To sum it up," said Doctor Rubin, "if my nephew read your revised work, would he feel glad that he had been born in the Soviet Union rather than, say, in the United States?"

"But of course!" Barkov exclaimed with sincere surprise. "I couldn't possibly convey any other attitude. Whatever its achievements, capitalism is based upon the philosophy of dog-eat-dog and the egocentricity of acquiring individual wealth. And whatever the shortcomings of socialism, it is based upon the ideals of human brotherhood and of the greatest good for the greatest number."

There was a pause, during which the two doctors exchanged a brief glance. Abruptly Doctor Rubin asked, "Just between ourselves, with false modesty put aside, do you consider yourself to be the most important contemporary Soviet writer?"

Barkov would have laughed at the transparency of the question if he had not regarded it as being so sinister.

"Certainly not."

"But why not? Your books have been published in large editions, haven't they?"

"A popular author does not necessarily write literature of the first rank."

"Not necessarily, but he may. Tolstoy was widely read – so also were Gorky, Hugo, Balzac.* Have your books been published in other countries?"

"Yes."

"Capitalist as well as socialist?"

"Four in capitalist countries, seven in the socialist ones."

"And I recall that several successful films and stage plays have been based on your work?"

"Yes, but written by others."

"You've also published some children's books in these last years?"

"Yes."

"And is there any other contemporary author who has written a book that is required reading for every student in secondary school?"

"I'm sure Sholokhov's *And Quiet Flows the Don** is required reading at some stage of the educational process."

"Yes, true, but Sholokhov has not been writing very much for some time. He's scarcely a contemporary writer. So, all in all, how do you regard yourself?"

Barkov asked quietly, "What answer would you like me to give?"

The question was disconcerting. Doctor Rubin adjusted his eyeglasses and exclaimed hastily, "Why, the truth, of course."

"I've already told you the truth. I don't consider myself to be the most important contemporary Soviet writer. But you seem to be trying to persuade me to say I am. Why are you?"

"You misunderstand," Doctor Larina put in gently. "If an individual underestimates his worth, it is as significant psychologically as if he overestimates it. I'm sure that Doctor Rubin's questions were designed to find out whether or not you have a normal sense of self-esteem."

"Yes, precisely," Doctor Rubin muttered. "For instance, I would like you to name a writer you consider more important than yourself."

CHAPTER 7

Since Barkov knew that the search of his apartment had turned up a manuscript copy of *The First Circle* as well as a framed photograph of its author, he replied at once, "Alexander Solzhenitsyn, for one. There are others as well."

"Hm, Solzhenitsyn! So if you were in charge of things, as it were, you would publish Solzhenitsyn's works?"

"Certainly. I think it shames us in the eyes of the whole world that we have published only his first work – which has, moreover, lately been removed from our libraries. Why should a great country be afraid of a few books?"

"Why should a socialist society spend the people's money on books hostile to socialism?"

"Solzhenitsyn's books are certainly hostile to the type of deformed socialism that Stalin instituted. In my eyes, to be anti-Stalinist is not to be anti-socialist."

"Well, I won't discuss so complex a question with you for the moment. But since you regard Solzhenitsyn so highly, I have a question. Last year he sent a letter to all delegates to the Writers' Congress. A certain number of them petitioned the Presidium for a discussion of the letter. How is it your name was not on that list?"

It was a simple question, but it abruptly exposed the fraudulence of this psychiatric examination. The smiling bitch opposite him had said that they had been ordered to examine him because someone unknown had reported that he had been behaving abnormally. Indeed, according to them they had not even known that he had been brought to the hospital by force. But now this Rubin bastard was asking him about a petition to a congress that had taken place in May of the previous year. Both of them had been briefed! Briefed and directed by the Security Police, who had kidnapped him! Behind this façade of a psychiatric examination he was being tested politically. That's why Rubin had wanted to know how he would revise his book.

"I didn't attend the congress, doctor. I was not a delegate."

"But if you had attended it, would you have signed the letter?"

"It's well over a year since I read it. I would like to see it again before I answer you."

"Are you aware that there is increasing discussion about expelling Solzhenitsyn from the Writers' Union?"

"Yes."

"If it is put to a vote, how will you stand on it?"

"Excuse me, but I don't understand why that question is relevant to a psychiatric examination."

"We evaluate the total individual," Doctor Larina told him. "There is nothing in your life that is irrelevant or may not be meaningful to us."

He kept the rancour out of his voice. "If I tell you that I am very fond of smoked eel... is that relevant?"

"It might be," Doctor Larina responded comfortably. "We would have to be the judge of that. Why don't you answer Doctor Rubin's question?"

"I can't know in advance how I will vote. I will have to listen to the discussion, if it ever comes before the Writers' Union." The lie was spoken easily in the face of the two hypocrites opposite him. But even though it was justifiable, he felt dirtied by it. The whole situation was insufferably filthy.

Doctor Larina said quietly, "Daniil Petrovich, would you be good enough to explain your attitude about the wearing of decorations? Most citizens, for instance, would take pride in wearing a Medal of Valour. And certainly the medal that accompanies the Lenin Prize! But apparently you leave your decorations in a bureau drawer. Why is that?"

"There's no law governing the matter, is there, Doctor Larina? And not even an accepted custom. Some citizens wear decorations at all times, some only on special occasions. May I ask the relevance of the question?"

"Yes, of course. If someone never wore his decorations, it might indicate that he was ashamed of them. The next question would be: 'Why?' Did he feel that he had not earned them

CHAPTER 7

honourably? Or had he lost self-esteem? Or had he perhaps become hostile to the Soviet system?"

"I no longer wear the medal that accompanied my Stalin Prize," Barkov replied slowly. "We can discuss the reasons for that, if you like. I wear my other decorations on important occasions like May Day or 7th November."

"But not in general?"

"No."

"That's a clear pattern, and quite normal. Tell me, do you feel that, if you were to speak out on a public matter, many people would be influenced by you?"

"I have no idea. It would depend on the topic, in what manner I discussed it, and under what circumstances. I am sure that if I wrote a letter to *Pravda* arguing that the earth was flat, not even a shepherd in Georgia would be persuaded."

"Well, let's talk about another kind of letter to *Pravda*." She lifted a briefcase from the floor. He recognized it as the one Number Three had been carrying. As he expected, she took out of it the pages he had written that morning. She placed them flat on the table and looked at him steadily for a moment. Her eyes were bright and searching.

"This 'Eyewitness Report'... you personally witnessed this event yesterday?"

"Yes."

"For whom were you writing it?"

"For *Pravda*. I intended to take it myself to the editorial office."

"Did you actually expect *Pravda* to publish it?"

"I hoped it would be published, naturally."

A knife edge of sarcasm altered the professional calm of her voice. "Daniil Petrovich, aren't you somewhat out of touch with reality? These demonstrators were attacking a major policy decision by our Party and government. They were behaving like paid agents of the CIA – for all either of us know, they may be. But you nevertheless expect *Pravda* to publish this report of yours which is full of sympathy for them? No wonder there have been reports of abnormal behaviour on your part!"

Barkov drew a deep breath and responded quietly. "If you will reread those pages, Doctor Larina, you will see that I express no support of the political position taken by the demonstrators. I merely point out that eight Soviet citizens were beaten and arrested for a peaceful act which is lawful. Article 125 of our Constitution guarantees citizens the right both of free expression and of freedom of public demonstration."

"And what if *Pravda* didn't publish your letter – what would you then do with it?"

"Submit it elsewhere – *Novy Mir*, the *Literary Gazette*,* and so on."

"And what if no newspaper or magazine would publish it?"

"Then I would put it on the shelf of rejected manuscripts well known to all writers."

"Why? Wouldn't there be other alternatives?"

"What?"

"Circulate it in manuscript form as Solzhenitsyn, the writer you so admire, whose photograph you have above your desk, does with his novels?"

"And perhaps," added Doctor Rubin, "slip it to some foreign journalists so that it would appear in the anti-Soviet newspapers of the West?"

"Those are your alternatives. They are not mine."

"You mean you never even considered them?" Doctor Larina asked sharply.

"No, I never considered them!"

"Despite the fact that you felt so deeply about the mistreatment of the demonstrators that you picked up two teeth that had fallen from the mouth of one of them?"

"Despite that fact, yes."

"How and when did you pick up the teeth?"

"After the demonstrators were taken away, and after the spectators dispersed, I happened to notice them."

CHAPTER 7

"You mean you didn't leave when the other spectators did?"

"No."

"Why not?"

"St Basil's was very beautiful with the bright sun on it. I remained looking at it. Then, when I was leaving, I noticed the teeth."

"Why did you pick them up? They were bloody, weren't they?"

He yearned to give her the same answer he had given Lidia the night before, but knew it would be unwise. With a shrug he replied, "Yes, they were bloody, but I'm an admirer of Chekhov. I'm trying to profit from his approach to writing."

"What does that mean?"

"In one of his letters he wrote that if you placed an object before him – a pair of scissors, a coffee cup or whatnot – and told him to write a story about it, he'd have one for you in twenty-four hours. Or perhaps it was forty-eight, I forget.* Since I already was thinking about writing a letter to *Pravda*, I picked up the teeth."

Doctor Larina gazed at him intently. "I see. Would it interest you to know that I called the KGB after reading your report?"

"Yes, it would."

"I was informed that the demonstration had indeed taken place. The demonstrator who was injured is named Viktor Fainberg. He is at this moment confined for examination in the Serbsky Institute of Forensic Psychiatry.* Would you like to know why?"

"Please."

"His injury was self-inflicted – he hit himself in the mouth with a stick."

The statement was so unexpected that Barkov was bellowing with laughter before he realized it. "Very good," he said after a bit, "the moon is made of caviar and no one but a mental case would dispute it."

"Will you be prepared to testify in a courtroom that the official of the Security Police was lying?"

"I will testify that either he was lying or else he was told a lie by a subordinate."

"And what if these individuals are put on trial and evidence is provided that they have secret political links with enemies of the Soviet Union?"

"I think that traitors to our country should be punished appropriately. But anyone who says that Fainberg knocked his own teeth out with a stick is a liar."

Doctor Larina nodded and glanced at her watch. "We'll now have a short interruption. I must have a quick visit with a patient." She pressed a buzzer under the table. The door opened, and Grigory was there. "Ten minutes," Doctor Larina told him. He nodded and gestured for Barkov to leave the room.

Striped pyjamas, fibre slippers and a so-called psychiatric examination, Barkov thought with fury. Silently he did as he was told. In the waiting room he asked Grigory if he could go to the toilet. The latter nodded and unlocked the door to the corridor. With a grin he said, "There are two main categories of mental patients: those who are constipated and those who have diarrhoea."

Barkov asked drily, "What psychiatric conclusion will be drawn from the fact that after tea and lemonade I need to piss?"

Grigory laughed. "That's serious, that needs looking into."

"Will you tell me what time it is?"

"Two ten."

"Thank you."

Anna was expecting him at four, but he believed now that he was hip-deep in a swamp and would not be walking out of it in an hour. His heart ached for Anna and what she would suffer when he didn't appear and could not be located. Yet there was a greater urgency: to think, to plan how to manoeuvre, to somehow perceive where this was leading! Doctor Bitch had

CHAPTER 7

said she needed a quick visit with a patient. More likely it was a quick conversation with the KGB agent in charge of his case. But what case, damn it? Shilova had said he had been charged with violation of the Criminal Code. *That*, it was clear, had been a falsehood designed solely to explain the search warrant. In effect he had been blindfolded, locked up, and now was being dissected politically by two psychiatrists. The suggestion already had been made that his thinking was out of touch with reality. Yet why hadn't he, like Fainberg, been taken directly to the Serbsky Institute, which processed legal psychiatric cases? Surely the reason was that he had done nothing overt. But, in that case, why was he here at all?

It was no good – he had had these same thoughts earlier. He was like a hamster on a wheel – racing frenetically but going nowhere.

2

The interruption lasted not ten, but twenty-five minutes. When the interview was resumed, Doctor Larina offered him another glass of lemonade. He thanked her politely and murmured, "Perhaps later." Doctor Rubin, with an unlit cigarette between his lips, was reading Shika's letter. Barkov reflected sourly that Shilova's search warrant had proved to be quite fruitful. Presently the cigarette was tapped on the table. Doctor Rubin asked coldly, "Has your friend ever been institutionalized for mental treatment?"

"No!" His snappish answer had been automatic, and he instantly told himself that it was stupid, utterly stupid, not to control his feelings. If he allowed these loathsome creatures to get under his skin, they would use his behaviour against him.

"When you read his letter, did nothing about it strike you as being pathological?"

Quietly: "No."

"But how can you be so blind? Your friend is a clear paranoid."

"On what do you base that conclusion?"

"The letter screams it from beginning to end."

Quietly again: "Doctor Rubin, if a Jew at Babi Yar* screamed just before being shot by the Nazis, was he under the delusion that he was being persecuted?"

"There is *nothing* comparable in the two situations!" Rubin replied with marked irritation. "Your friend says he was dismissed from the army. I accept that as a probable fact. But no one has slapped his face, imprisoned him or shot him. To the contrary, he has been given a pension! As to the real reason for his dismissal, I am positive he is covering up his own failures when he cries anti-Semitism. The Polish government is anti-Zionist as I myself am strongly anti-Zionist. But that is not the same as being anti-Semitic, which I obviously could not be. Your friend is a paranoid!"

It had not occurred to Barkov before this that Rubin was Jewish. The latter's irritation, however, and his arbitrary dismissal of Shika's letter, revealed it. It had been quite some years back, shortly before Stalin's death, that Shika had provided him with a compassionate understanding of what he called "the lapdog Jew". Shika, that irreligious, dedicated Communist, had said that he, like others, would proclaim himself a Jew so long as a single anti-Semite remained on earth. But there were some Jews who wished they had been born almost anything else. In response to the open and veiled pressures against them in Soviet society, they grasped at security by offering fanatical loyalty to every Kremlin policy. They espoused the righteous cause of the Arab nations, and were indifferent to the abused Jews of so many countries who had found Israel the only refuge open to them in the world. Whatever Rubin's professional and social status, there was a corrosive fear in his heart – and there was no possibility of carrying on a rational discussion with him about Shika's letter.

"Well?" Doctor Rubin asked. "What have you got to say now?"

CHAPTER 7

"You've made your diagnosis. I have nothing to say."

Doctor Larina spoke up with some sharpness. "Daniil Petrovich, this is not a situation in which we can permit evasion. What do you believe *now* about your friend's letter?"

Very calmly: "Inasmuch as I've known him intimately for twenty-three years, I believe that what he wrote me is the truth."

"Therefore," she continued, "like your hero, Solzhenitsyn, you consider it your duty to circulate a manuscript in which you repeat these so-called facts about Poland?"

"Excuse me – I have not said anything about circulating a manuscript!"

"Wasn't that your intention?"

"No."

"Are you positive?"

"Yes, positive."

Doctor Larina nodded and turned her attention to the briefcase on her desk.

What next? Barkov wondered with anger. Would they ask why he had a cubist print by Picasso on his wall? If Picasso were a Soviet citizen, he would be excluded from the Artists' Union and could be tried as a parasite who did no socially useful work.

Doctor Larina drew a manuscript that had been typed on onion-skin paper from the briefcase. She read aloud: "*Progress, Coexistence and Intellectual Freedom* by Andrei D. Sakharov.* You acknowledge that this was in your apartment?"

"'Acknowledge' is not quite the word. I affirm it!"

Her eyebrows raised a little. "Are you a friend of academician Sakharov?"

"Unfortunately I never met him."

"How did you get the manuscript?"

"It was given to me by a friend."

"What friend?"

"If I tell you, it may result in his being kidnapped and locked up in a mental institution!" He was sorry the moment he snapped it out, but decided that it would be an error to apologize.

"We're accustomed to hostile remarks," Doctor Larina said with a tiny smile. "It doesn't affect our desire to help the patient we're dealing with."

"I'm aware that you are questioning me politically, but I have yet to perceive any way in which you are helping me – aside from the fact that I haven't asked for your help and don't need it."

"Mental illness takes various forms. We investigate the total personality."

"Besides," Doctor Rubin added, "it's already clear that in certain respects you are incapable of looking at your own behaviour with objectivity."

Barkov's hands gripped his thighs. "Before this moment no one ever suggested that I was mentally ill. For the past month I have been going to the hospital every day to see my wife. I have spoken to doctors and nurses. Why didn't they notice anything about me?"

"How do you know they didn't?" Doctor Larina asked with a comfortable smile. "The chief psychiatrist received reports about you from somewhere. Besides, the symptoms of mental illness can vary in intensity from hour to hour or day to day. Sometimes they can be so well concealed that only specialists like us can perceive them."

"Or witch doctors!" Barkov snapped.

"There, another hostile remark! Have you always distrusted physicians?"

"To the contrary! But I never before met physicians who subjected me to a political inquisition."

"Dear Daniil Petrovich, if you could only realize that we can't help you unless we thoroughly understand you... A man's political views are an important part of his personality."

He wanted to shout, "Shove your help up your arse, you hypocrite," but forced himself to remain silent.

CHAPTER 7

"Why do you think the Sakharov book was not published?" she continued in a patient tone.

"Because the censorship imposed on us is stupid," Barkov responded passionately. "It cripples the growth of socialism! One of the most precious gifts any citizen can offer his country is a new idea. When Sakharov's ideas contributed to the development of the hydrogen bomb, he was honoured. But when he wrote a small book with some new ideas on social problems, he could not get it published. It's completely stupid!"

"Sakharov is a scientist of great prestige," Doctor Rubin observed. "Has it occurred to you that the decision not to publish his book was made not by a run-of-the-mill censor, but by the highest Party authorities?"

"Then all the worse for our country!" Barkov snapped.

There... it was out and to hell with them!

A door behind Doctor Rubin was thrust open. A chunky, stony-bald man in his late fifties entered. He sat down beside Doctor Larina and put a portfolio on the table. He gazed at Barkov with a slight smile. It was not a friendly smile: it seemed to say, "I know all about you, chum." He was formidable-looking – his features strong, his blue eyes piercing.

"I am Doctor Kulagin," he announced in a stern voice.

Barkov realized with a jolt that he now was facing a commission of three doctors who had the power to declare him to be mentally incompetent.

"Where were you on the fifth of December of last year at six o'clock in the evening?" Kulagin asked sharply.

The fifth of December was Constitution Day. Barkov knew instantly that he must have been observed in the small crowd on Pushkin Square.

"I was on Pushkin Square."

"Did you go there with anyone?"

"I decline to answer."

"You went there with your friend, Professor Ilya Krasny, a member of the Human Rights Committee. Why did you go?"

"Out of curiosity – one of the characteristics of an author. Since you know I was there, you ought to know also that I didn't bare my head when the others did."

"That is correct, but you *were there*, so don't play games with me. You know what I know: those yearly demonstrations didn't begin until the arrest in '65 of those two anti-Soviet scribblers, Sinyavsky and Daniel. By attending as a spectator last year, you were supporting the slogan of that silent demonstration."

"I didn't know what the slogan was, and I didn't bare my head."

"You didn't bare your head for some tactical reason of your own, but you knew damn well what the slogan was! It was the insulting assertion that socialist justice is punishing innocent people."

"Has it never?"

"The Stalin days are over!" Doctor Kulagin shouted with unmistakable indignation. "Socialist legality has been completely restored!"

Very quietly Barkov asked, "Then why am I here? I have been illegally deprived of my liberty – a serious crime in which you seem to be participating."

"Nonsense! You are here because you have been showing grave signs of both mental instability and antisocial behaviour."

"Signs? What signs, please?"

Kulagin took a photograph out of his portfolio and thrust it forward. "You are standing only one metre behind your friend, Krasny, who was warned yesterday by the KGB that, if he continues his public activity, he not only will be dismissed from his post at Moscow University, but will not be allowed to work anywhere else in the field of chemistry. He can drive a taxi or sell fish."

Barkov felt a lump of anguish and anger forming in his throat. Ilya had hoped that it was only a threat, but they meant it!

"You also are standing less than three metres away from Pavel Litvinov and Larisa Danielova, who were arrested yesterday

CHAPTER 7

on Red Square for hooliganism and are now in custody. You are standing no more than five metres away from that alcoholic troublemaker, Pyotr Yakir,* and that mental case, Grigorenko, who by his behaviour is paving his way back* to an institution."

"I am a writer!" Barkov half shouted with a heat he could not temper. "I am entitled to observe what goes on in my country. I've already told you that one of my tools is curiosity."

"Yes, curiosity," Kulagin echoed acidly. "You went to Pushkin Square solely out of curiosity. But in this photograph you are wearing both the Medal of Valour and the Lenin Prize Medal. You told Doctor Larina you only wore them on special occasions."

"Isn't Constitution Day a special occasion? I like our Constitution. I believe we have an excellent Constitution."

"What a clever man you are!" Kulagin dropped the photograph on the table. "Are you a secret member of the Human Rights Committee?"

"No."

"On the eleventh of January of this year you withdrew seven hundred and fifty roubles from your account in the savings bank in the Hotel Ukraina. On that same day, your friend Ilya Krasny deposited the identical sum in his account in the same bank. Was that your money?"

Barkov felt the blood rushing to his head. This meant that he had been under close surveillance by the KGB since Constitution Day. "Yes, it was."

"Why did you give him so much money?"

"It was a personal loan."

"For what purpose?"

"He didn't tell me, and I didn't enquire. We've been close friends since childhood."

"Isn't it a fact that he asked you for funds to assist in the publication of the *Chronicle of Current Events*?"

"As I've told you, it was a personal loan."

"The first two issues of the *Chronicle* were found in your apartment. From whom did you get them?"

"I won't tell you."

"Were copies of it typed on your typewriter or on your wife's for further circulation?"

"No."

"When Doctor Larina asked what you would do if no newspaper or magazine would publish your 'Eyewitness Report', you said you would put it on your shelf of rejected manuscripts. Is that correct?"

"Yes."

"But that was a lie, wasn't it?"

"No, it was not a lie."

"When she asked whether you intended to circulate a manuscript based on the letter from your Polish friend, Botwin, you said you did not. But that also was a lie, wasn't it?"

"No, it was not."

There was a long pause as Doctor Kulagin stared at Barkov with his blue eyes on fire with anger. "How is it then that last evening you told your mistress, Lidia Karpova, that you intended to circulate your 'Eyewitness Report' in manuscript form, and that from one end of our country to the other people were going to read about the persecution of Botwin?"

Not since the war, not since the last time a heavy shell exploded close by him, had Barkov experienced an equivalent shock. As with a shell blast that was too much for his senses to contain, he was left stupefied. He had no thoughts or feelings: his eyes stopped seeing, his ears stopped hearing – he remained mute.

Chapter 8

I

Barkov found that he was alone in the room, but didn't know how long he had been alone. He had not heard Doctor Kulagin tell him a few moments earlier that a bit of reflection might do him good. He had emerged from his brief, catatonic peace to the torture of too much feeling, of too many contradictory thoughts and questions that could not be resolved. He felt as though he was bleeding internally.

How had Kulagin known what he had told Lidia? It now was clear that since the fifth of December he had been under the surveillance of the Security Police. Therefore, when he and Lidia became lovers, they probably had installed microphones in her apartment. Surely there were microphones in his apartment also – and in his Peredelkino home as well. If that was so, if they had a tape recording of all of his conversations with both Anna and Lidia...

The thought was overwhelming. His mind could accept the possibility, but his emotions rejected it. And there was something else: could he be certain – absolutely certain – that the microphones had been installed without Lidia's knowledge? The KGB had informers everywhere. How did he know?...

Of course he could be certain, of course! It was nonsense to even think of Lidia as an informer.

Nonsense? If it were Anna, it *would* be nonsense. But in reality, looking truth in the face, how well did he know Lidia? He knew her as a vibrant, engaging companion – he knew the wine of her lips and breasts and the sweet cries of passion deep in her throat – but she could be an informer despite that. They had been together less than a month. What did he really know of her past? Or of entanglements that could have enmeshed her so deeply that even against her will she had had to report their conversation of last evening to the KGB? Indeed, she might have reported it without knowing it would be used in a way that would expose her. How could he be sure about her in his inner heart the way a man *had* to be sure?

Barkov groaned. He didn't believe it, but was there any way in which he ever would know with certainty? Was it only this morning that he had thought with such happiness of their having a child together? The morning was a light year away – the thought already polluted by maggots of suspicion.

How awful it was, how wounding, how inexpressibly painful!

The door was opened by Doctor Kulagin, who stared at him for a long moment before entering. The two others followed. Barkov shivered with rage at seeing them. He turned his eyes towards the patch of grey sky. Doctor Kulagin said, "I observe before me a man whose talent..." He paused. "I suggest that the patient give me his attention."

Turning, Barkov snapped, "I am not a patient, I am a prisoner!"

"To us you are a patient in need of help, and you had better listen to me with care. I repeat that I observe before me with a clinical eye a man whose talent has made a contribution to the cultural life of his country. For this reason, he has been honoured in various ways by his fellow citizens and by his government. For years he has enjoyed the best our society has to offer: awards and honours, a fine apartment, a splendid country home, an automobile, royalties that were more than enough for him to live well and to travel. This man also knows that his chronically ill wife has received expert medical and hospital care at no financial cost. In the light of all of this, I, as a psychiatrist, am forced to say that when such a man turns against his government, he *must* be mentally unbalanced."

CHAPTER 8

With intensity Barkov retorted, "I love my country, but I would also like to love justice. I have *not* turned against my government, but it was not just, and it was a violation of our Constitution, for the eight demonstrators to be physically abused and arrested yesterday morning."

"The demonstrators will be investigated, and, if necessary, will be tried in court," Kulagin responded calmly. "If they are innocent of violating the law, they will be set free. But you don't know and I don't know what foreign connections they may have, or how much they may have been paid to go to Red Square. If you wish—"

Barkov interrupted with a quietly scornful question. "How much money do you suppose Litvinov, the physicist, would require of his foreign connections to spend some years in a Siberian penal camp?"

Kulagin went on as though Barkov had not spoken. "If you wish to complete your 'Eyewitness Report' and send it to the Public Prosecutor's Office for examination, you are free to do so. But to circulate it in manuscript form as you intend means that it will arrive in the West and will be used by our enemies against us. This we are—"

"Oh, yes, our dangerous foreign enemies!" Barkov interrupted again. "One can find some basis for Stalin's paranoia since our country did have enemies capable of destroying her in its early years. But who can destroy the Soviet Union now? No nation in the world, no combination of nations! Yet you still make use of the same whip: our foreign enemies."

"There are ideological as well as physical enemies to contend with," Doctor Kulagin responded forcefully. "We are not going to allow you to provide our enemies in the West with ideological aid."

"Is it illegal to circulate manuscripts?" Barkov asked sharply.

"It is illegal if they contain fabrications, yes."

"My report will contain no fabrications!"

"Whether or not it will, you are not going to circulate it. It is a sign of serious mental instability when a citizen of your prominence does not even weigh the shame of having the Voice of America gleefully broadcast something he has written. You have been a symbol of patriotism for too many years to too many of our people. You will remain a symbol! You are not going to force us to withdraw your books from our libraries and schools. We will not allow you to join the ranks of corrupt renegades like Sakharov, Yakir, Grigorenko and Solzhenitsyn!"

With choking rage Barkov shouted, "You are not going to allow me? What does that mean?"

"Let's be very open," Doctor Rubin put in sharply. "You intended to circulate a polemic about your Polish friend. You boasted to Lidia Karpova that you would arouse public opinion from here to Vladivostok. Through the power of your pen our government would be forced to interfere in Polish internal affairs so that Botwin would be restored to his post in the army. Now, what do my colleagues think? Are there some delusions of grandeur here?"

"Not only that, but there are other signs of pathology," Doctor Larina said earnestly. "The patient has forgotten that a global battle is being fought for the mind and soul of humanity. Until that battle is won, every Soviet writer must be a soldier defending his people against imperialist ideology. The patient's intention of circulating self-published manuscripts is a clear sign of a split in his personality. On the one hand he is a genuine patriot, on the other he is ready to be used by our enemies. Therefore, it is our obligation, as psychiatrists, to protect him from the abnormalities that have developed in his character."

Barkov jumped to his feet. "Exactly what are you threatening?"

"Threatening?" Doctor Kulagin responded calmly. "No one *ever* is threatened here. When signs of mental illness become apparent, a patient is treated to restore him to health. In your case we already have a tentative diagnosis, but further observation is necessary."

CHAPTER 8

"And what does that mean?" Barkov shouted.

"Daniil Petrovich, you surely are not so ill that you don't know the meaning of what I just said?"

"Does it mean you are going to keep me here by force?"

"We cannot observe you if you are not here to be observed."

"So you think it will be easy to keep me locked up?" Barkov shouted violently. "I'll remind you that it wasn't many months ago that the mathematician Yesenin-Volpin was incarcerated in a mental hospital for his lawful activities as a citizen. The cruel fraud was exposed when ninety-five of our leading academicians signed a statement asserting their positive knowledge of his mental health. Do you think there won't be hundreds of our leading writers, artists and scientists who will sign for me?"

"February is not August," Kulagin remarked icily. "Czechoslovakia has shown our government how easily mush-headed intellectuals can depart from the path of socialism. This interview is over!" He pressed a button under the desk.

"You think you won't be exposed?" Barkov cried hoarsely. "You think this won't blow up in your face?"

Grigory stepped into the room.

"To be held for observation," said Doctor Kulagin. He rose and walked out of the room. Doctors Larina and Rubin followed.

"Now then," said Grigory in a stone-hard voice, "I heard enough shouting to know that you're very angry. So take some deep breaths and cool down a bit. Otherwise you'll give me trouble and you'll regret it!"

Grigory had read Barkov's mind. The instant the doctors started out of the room, the flash thought had come that this was the moment to try an escape. Grigory was a bigger man, younger, and undoubtedly trained to subdue violent patients. But Barkov was strong, in good physical shape, and he had not forgotten all of the wrestling he had learnt as a university student. The element of surprise was on his side. If he started out of the room in a meek manner, he could suddenly jump

Grigory and slam him to the floor. But what would come next? Unless he instantly beat him unconscious, Grigory would struggle and yell for help. Yet suppose he did silence him? Was the key to the outside door in his pocket? Where was that door?... He didn't know the geography of the hospital. He couldn't go wandering around the halls in the uniform of a patient. To put on Grigory's clothes would mean...

"Well, now, let's go, eh?" Grigory said, and gestured for Barkov to move first.

In the waiting room there was a second orderly, someone he had not seen before.

The bastards have everything thought out in advance, Barkov reflected with sick anger.

2

The room was small and stuffy, and he took off his robe. High up on one white wall there was a tiny, barred, open window that looked out on a brick wall only two metres away. He could see some light, but no sky. Below the window there was an electric bulb behind a thick glass that was flush with the surface of the wall. The furnishings of the room were a canvas cot with a thin mattress and a two-litre can that smelt of cleaning fluid. The heavy wooden door had a peephole in it that could be opened from the outside only.

They had put him in a cage so that he could be observed. But for how long?

How long? He had been kidnapped – were there any restraints on their power? No one knew where he was, no one would know tomorrow or the day after. He had threatened Kulagin with hundreds of signatures of protest, but who would sign what? In the case of Yesenin-Volpin it had been quite different. He had been openly arrested, subjected to a formal psychiatric examination – however farcical – and then formally sentenced by a court to compulsory treatment in an institution. But since

CHAPTER 8

there was nothing open and formal about *his* case, what could anyone find out about him?

His thoughts went to his wife. He guessed that it was about three fifteen or three thirty. In another hour Anna would become apprehensive and would ask a nurse to telephone for her. By six o'clock she would be frantically asking friends and the hospital director to assist her. But there would be no official knowledge of his whereabouts and no record of his having been admitted to the emergency ward of any hospital. In Peredelkino neighbours would not find him at his home. The militia would ask if he was a heavy drinker. They would enquire whether there was any possibility that he had fallen into the river while walking along the embankment. If so, the body would float to the surface in a few days.

What *was* going to happen to him here? Kulagin had said they would not *allow* him to circulate his 'Eyewitness Report'. How could they prevent it? Were they thinking of keeping him locked up until he promised not to write it? A promise extracted under duress was meaningless. He would repudiate it the moment he was at liberty, and he would bring criminal charges against them with the backing of the Writers' Union. What a scandal there would be when he told his story at the Writers' Club! There would be an immediate written protest to the Central Committee of the Party, with hundreds and hundreds of signatures.

Barkov swung around as a key turned noisily in the door lock. Kolya came in carrying a tray. The door was closed by someone unseen in the corridor.

"Hello, how are you?" Kolya asked in an anxious manner. "I brought you some food. Even if you're not hungry, you'd better eat – you didn't have much lunch." He stepped over to the cot and set the tray down. "Come on, sit down. I want to talk to you."

Beware of this smooth bastard, Barkov told himself – and, of course, of the microphone somewhere in the room! He sat down. Kolya had brought him bread, some slices of sausage, tea, two lumps of sugar. To his surprise he felt like eating. He moved the tray onto his knees.

"Comrade, I'm worried about you," Kolya told him. "I hear things didn't go so good for you."

"What can happen to me?" Barkov enquired calmly. "I haven't violated any law."

"You don't seem to understand. If a loony commits a crime, naturally he's sentenced to a mental institution. However, suppose a man doesn't commit a crime but he's mentally off-balance? For instance, he's depressed and talking about suicide. His family gets worried and reports it. In that case, a commission of three psychiatrists can lock him up."

"But I'm not depressed," Barkov replied lightly as he chewed a slice of sausage. "I'm not anxious – I was found to be neurologically healthy by a doctor in this hospital, and there is nothing bizarre about my behaviour. So what have I got to worry about?"

Kolya shook his head. "Chum," he said sadly, "you're like a little kitten with its eyes closed. From the way I heard it, there's already a diagnosis about your case: schizophrenia with delusions of grandeur. That's enough to keep you locked up."

"I can prove to a court that I'm sane."

"Hold on, chum, you've got the law all wrong!" Kolya said pityingly. "When a man commits a crime, it becomes a court case, sure. But with no crime involved, there's no court and no lawyer – the commission of three psychiatrists decides everything. If they say you need to be an inpatient, there's no higher authority to appeal to. Every month or three months you'll get examined again. If the commission doesn't think you've improved, you stay locked up. Like I said, there's no appeal. They can keep you locked up for years – for ever, if they like."

Barkov continued eating. His calm was genuine and was based upon the conviction that Kolya had not come to his room by accident. Kulagin, the son of a bitch, was trying to frighten him. He didn't care whether Kolya's exposition of the law was accurate. Probably it was, because it fitted what he recalled of General Grigorenko's case in '64. For repeatedly criticizing the Party leadership *in writing* Grigorenko had been kept in a mental institution for fifteen months. But what had *he* done of a like nature to anger the authorities? Nothing! His 'Eyewitness Report' was an unfinished five pages that he had not circulated. He had not put anything down on paper about Shika. The current Party leadership acted harshly against open political dissenters, but it still acted according to its laws. It might bend those laws a bit, as all governments did when expediency prompted. But in his case there was no law to be bent. The psychiatrists were bluffing, and that's why they had sent Kolya to him.

"Thank you for the information," he said lightly, "but it doesn't apply to me. Too many influential people know that I am not mentally unbalanced. It will not be possible to lock up Daniil Barkov."

"Like a three-day-old kitten," Kolya repeated with the same sad expression on his face and the same wag of his head. "You're at a crossroad in your life and you don't know it. To get out of here all you have to do is tell Doctor Kulagin that you don't intend to imitate those loony troublemakers like Yakir and Sakharov. You do that and..." – he snapped his fingers – "you'll be out of here and back to your good life. But keep up like you're doing and..." – again he snapped his fingers – "by tomorrow night you can be three hundred kilometres from here in the prison hospital at Oryol. That's where I told you I worked for two days. Those places can turn anyone mad. Just picture yourself with six others in a small cell, one bunk on top of the other, no room to turn around. One of those six could be like that disgusting loony we saw today who was picking at himself. Another could be violent, an insane brute who maybe stabbed his whole family and keeps threatening to choke you to death, so that you're afraid to sleep at night.

Or another could let out a scream every ten minutes day and night so you can't sleep. And that's just the beginning of it. Watery cabbage soup and rotting fish heads – that's your food, day in and day out. Toilets that are holes in the floor, stinking cesspits. No letters, no visits. And who are the orderlies? Why, they're regular criminals with the right to beat you up for any least thing. And if you complain to the doctors, they inject you with drugs till you turn into a vegetable. That's the other road, chum! I'm trying to warn you. By the time your friends find out where you are – if they ever do – that's what you'll be: a vegetable!"

Barkov shivered a little inside, but with outward calm ate the last piece of bread and sipped his tea. "I appreciate your trying to help me, Kolya. But I have faith in the justice of Soviet law. I don't believe I'll be sent to one of those prisons."

"Well, anyway," said Kolya, "this is just between the two of us, eh? I would get in trouble if you reported what I told you."

"Of course I won't tell. I'm glad to have a friend in here."

Kolya took the tray. "Best of luck. I'm going home and listen to some jazz. If you need anything like going to the toilet, just bang on the door. There's always an orderly outside."

"Thank you."

Kolya kicked the door twice. After a few moments it was opened.

3

Lying on his cot with his head on his hands Barkov mulled over the fact that Kolya had been instructed to try and frighten him. It was a sign of the weakness of Kulagin's position. Nevertheless, he still was locked up. Undoubtedly he was facing unpleasant hours – even days – of confinement. It made him want to smash faces.

It struck him suddenly that he was experiencing in the flesh what he and Anna had discussed philosophically on more than

CHAPTER 8

one occasion: that all of mankind lived in one sort of cage or another. The concept first had come to him in a bizarre way. Of all the letters he ever had received about his books, the most touching one had been signed by two Greeks who lived in the city of Piraeus. Their letter had been written in competent French, and he had received it in the late fall of '65. The men said that they had been released only recently from a concentration camp after eighteen years of imprisonment. This immediately identified them as Communist Party members. They wrote that for most of their eighteen years they had not been allowed to have either newspapers or books. However, in the several years before their release conditions had become easier, and they had been permitted reading materials. A friend in Marseilles had sent them the French edition of his novel *The Homecoming*. They had cherished it so much that they had translated it into Greek. Not only that, but several handwritten copies had been made of it, so that all five hundred prisoners in their island camp could read it. They were writing him now to ask if he would allow them to seek a publisher for their translation.

He had been profoundly moved and had written at once, not only giving his permission, but telling them that any royalties were to go to them. At Christmas time, '66, he sent them a card, but did not receive one in response. In February, however, his card was returned. Stamped on the envelope in French were the words "Address Unknown". It surprised and confused him. Why should they have moved without leaving a forwarding address?

He learnt why two months later, when a fascist military group took power in Greece in a violent coup that saw thousands arrested. His two friends either had disappeared into the underground ahead of time or else were once again in prison. Since then, he had not heard from them.

It was after this that he had begun to make notes for his thesis. On the streets of Calcutta whole families made their homes on sidewalks and in alleys. To beg, eat scraps, have sexual intercourse, give birth and die on a sidewalk was indeed to be in a cage. There was no poverty like that in the Soviet Union, but on the other hand Fainberg was now in a cage in the Serbsky Institute, and the other demonstrators in a different cage.

And what of the tiger cages of Saigon, where Viet Cong prisoners were held? Or the trade unionists in Spanish jails, and the blacks under the rule of apartheid in South Africa?

There was no place on earth in which there were no cages – and the most privileged of individuals were not exempt. The British banker, the Soviet factory manager or ballet dancer, the American industrialist, were all in an ecological cage. The eleven-mile envelope of oxygen that surrounded the earth was being chemically altered and depleted. Rivers and oceans were being polluted by both socialist and capitalist nations. His friend, Ilya, a thoughtful scientist, had said more than once that he doubted that the destruction of the earth's hygienic system was capable of being reversed.

Although he was not a scientist, the thesis of his essay would be to the contrary – that humanity could continue, that it could halt its self-destruction, but that it could do so only through informed, united effort to achieve intelligent goals. There was a story told about Karl Marx that fitted perfectly. It was said that his daughters had asked him to sum up the essence of life in one word. Marx had answered: "Struggle."*

It fitted his thesis. His Greek friends in prison, a black youth in Harlem, a Soviet scientist viewing with dismay the pollution of the Volga river – all in common had only one path to emancipation: intelligent, informed, united struggle against the evils in their environment. Whether they *would* struggle was not certain. Whether they would succeed was not certain. But only to the degree that men struggled to burst out of the cages in which they found themselves could they be considered free human beings. All others were in bondage.

CHAPTER 8

As for himself, he was in a cage, and the KGB was trying to bludgeon him into silence. The KGB would fail. He already was a dissenter, and he *would* become a Signer!

The key sounded noisily in the lock. Barkov continued to lie on the cot until he saw that the visitor was Doctor Larina. He got up silently.

"How are you feeling?" she enquired with a warm smile.

He shrugged and remained silent. He noticed that the peephole in the door was open, and that an eye was peering in at them. He noticed also that her white medical coat was unbuttoned, disclosing in part the outlines of her full breasts. Her superb beauty made him even more furious with her than if she had been ugly, as though she had even less right than an unprepossessing woman to allow the KGB to use her. It made no logical sense, but somehow she was more of a prostitute for being good-looking.

"I wonder if you know my husband – Professor Dmitry Larin, the philologist?"

His reply was blandly cool. "I've never met him. I read one of his articles some years ago."

"He considers you one of our finest authors."

"I'm pleased to hear it."

"That's why I have a personal as well as a professional interest in you. I've read everything you've written. I especially like your short stories. And my children adore what you've written for youngsters."

Barkov nodded politely and remained silent. The bitch was leading up to something.

"Because I respect you so much, I want to admit frankly that I did participate in a few innocent deceptions today. For instance, I did know that you had been brought to the hospital by force. But the deceptions were necessary. For instance, it was urgent to find out if you were suffering from emotional problems or if you were a member of an organized anti-Soviet group."

"Since you're a member of the Security Police," Barkov said lightly, "how is it you don't wear a tailored blue uniform beneath your white coat? It would set off your figure so attractively."

"You're angry, of course," she replied with a smile, "but I don't take offence. I am not a member of the KGB, but the Party and all of its organs are beacon lights that I follow."

Whether she was speaking the truth made no difference, and that was the horror of it! If she were merely a cynical careerist working for position, privilege and the special blue envelope of roubles that came to her monthly above her official salary, she was corrupt in one way. But if she was a neo-Stalinist who believed sincerely that the ethics of a psychiatrist could be dictated by a KGB bureaucrat, she was equally corrupt... in a different way, that was all.

"As a physician," she continued, "I see no difference between an alcoholic factory worker who hates the police (and therefore is a potential assassin) and an outstanding intellectual who sets himself against the Party leadership (and thereby is a potential counter-revolutionary). These are merely stages of the same type of illness. A psychiatrist is obliged to diagnose the disease, and begin treatment, at the earliest possible moment."

Barkov was suddenly weary of listening to this pap. He remembered a passage in one of Lenin's works in which he had written that the illusion that the bosses know everything best was a thesis enshrined naturally by officials.* The impulse to quote it to her withered at the thought of the ready philistine reply that would come with a lovely smile from those lovely lips.

"Well, and what did you and the Security Police find out about me?" he asked bluntly.

"I'm happy to say the conclusion is that you are not a member of an organized anti-Soviet group. Regrettably, however, you have tendencies leading you in that direction. Therefore, you must be kept for further observation until your treatment is decided upon." She reached into her pocket, took out a metal

CHAPTER 8

box and opened it. "Meanwhile, I'm going to give you an injection to calm your nerves."

"I'm perfectly calm, I don't need an injection."

She took out a hypodermic syringe already filled with liquid. She fitted a needle to it that was topped by a ball of cotton. "This was ordered by Doctor Kulagin."

"I refuse to be injected! Do you hear me? I refuse!"

"Daniil Petrovich," she said gently and sorrowfully, "you are an intelligent man. Do you really want me to summon orderlies and have you forcibly tied down? Doctor Kulagin wants to be sure that you will be at your best tomorrow. If you are not at ease, you won't have a good night's rest." She waited, hypodermic in hand.

"Very well," he said bitterly and angrily. "A prisoner has no choice. But I warn you that the public and the authorities will hear about this. I will not be silent."

"A prisoner must serve a definite sentence," she told him quietly. "A patient is sent home as soon as he recovers. You are not a prisoner. I expect you to be able to return to your home very soon. Please lower your pyjama bottom."

He obeyed. She swabbed a spot on his right buttock with cotton. He smelt the alcohol. The injection burned. She swabbed the spot again. By the time he had tied his pyjama bottom, she was at the open door.

"What did you inject me with? I'd like to know."

"Sulfazin* – a one per cent sterile solution in peach oil." She was not smiling now. Her hazel eyes were regarding him steadily and gravely. "It's a very helpful drug. We use it in certain special cases of progressive paralysis, or in very serious cases of schizophrenia – or in cases like yours. Goodnight."

She left without a smile. The door closed. The key grated. The spyhole was closed.

Barkov stood in troubled confusion, trying to make sense of her final remark. What did "cases like yours" mean? What did that look on her face indicate? He felt inexplicably uneasy.

The first verse of a poem came to his mind. It was one that had moved him so deeply that he had memorized it years before.

> Just because you did not give up your hopes for the
> world, for your country and for humanity...
> > they either send you to the gallows
> > or put you in jail
> > for ten years, for fifteen years
> > or, who cares, for even longer.*

Why had it popped into his mind now? It had been written by Nâzım Hikmet, a Communist poet who had spent thirteen years in a Turkish prison. Ill with coronary-artery disease, he finally had been released and had come to the Soviet Union. When Hikmet had written "they put you in jail", he had been referring to the semi-fascist rulers of a capitalist country. But now he, Barkov, was using "they" for the Communist bureaucrats who were keeping him in this cage.

Yet these very bureaucrats, and their predecessors, had provided many other freedoms for the people of the Soviet Union. He had written about this with passion in his *Letters to a Foreign Journalist*. The well-born in a rich society took for granted their freedom from periodic famine, from lice, from malaria, from illiteracy. They took for granted also their freedom to get an education, to rise in their society, to enjoy literature, theatre, ballet, film. Under the tsars these freedoms had existed for a thin upper crust of the population, but had been denied to the people at large. Even in a cage, these matters had to be weighed.

It was warm in the room. He took off his pyjama top and tossed it on the cot. Then he went to the door and struck it twice with his fist. There was no response. As he struck it a third time, the peephole opened. A pale-blue eye looked at him, and a deep bass voice asked, "What do you want?"

"I need to go to the toilet."

CHAPTER 8

"To do what?"

"Piss."

"Use the can – that's what it's for. When it's almost full, let me know."

With distaste Barkov used the can, but he smiled slightly at how far he had come from the boy who had lived his first years in a clapboard-and-log house. One never walked to the outhouse on an icy night. The odours of a chamber pot had been a normal part of the long winters.

It was warm, very warm. It must be getting on to five o'clock. Poor Anna would be frantic by now. He rubbed the spot on his buttock where the needle had stabbed him. The slight burning caused by the injection had not gone away: it was becoming a rather painful spot.

Anna, Anna! It was so unfair that she should have any additional pain! He recalled something she once told him. Not long before President Kennedy was assassinated, he had said, "Life is not fair."* Anna didn't know whether the remark was original with him or whether he had borrowed it from someone else, but for her it was philosophic meat.

He remembered her delight on the last morning they had been together at Peredelkino. She was a birdwatcher, and she had come to him with shining eyes to report that finally, finally, she had witnessed something she had read about but never seen: two birds kissing. When he went to the front door, he saw it himself: two small birds he didn't recognize touching and intertwining their open beaks. Since he had no great interest in birds, it was Anna's shining eyes that had made the occasion memorable, her lovely grey eyes gleaming again with youthful joy in a face turned old by illness.

"Oh, Anna, Anna, Anna!" he thought with sorrow as he wiped the perspiration off his brow. The indelible memory of one of their early days together came to mind. It was the seventh of November 1941, the twenty-fourth anniversary of the Revolution. He, Anna and an elderly man were on the roof of her apartment house hammering boards over a hole where a firebomb had struck the night before. It was a cold, grey morning with an unusual number of their planes patrolling the city. They could hear in the distance the steady pounding of heavy artillery. Suddenly an announcement came over the loudspeaker on the street below them – that Stalin was standing on Lenin's Tomb with other Party leaders! Stalin was about to address fresh troops who would march directly from Red Square to the front.

It was electrifying. In the weeks past whole ministries of government had been removed to Kuybyshev.* But Stalin was in Red Square! Stalin had not fled, and therefore Moscow would not fall!

And then Stalin began to speak in his flat monotone with its Georgian accent, calling for indomitable struggle, giving assurance that the invaders would be defeated. At that moment the pulse of more than two hundred million citizens had beat in time with Stalin's pulse. In the four terrible years of war that followed there were millions of soldiers like himself who had advanced in an attack with the shout "For Stalin!"

And yet human emotions were so complex that above all else that had occurred on that historic morning he recalled the beautiful luminosity of Anna's deep grey eyes as she listened to the voice on the loudspeaker.

He didn't feel well. He was perspiring more than seemed reasonable, and the injection point in his right buttock felt painful. He felt a bit weak, and headachy also. What was wrong with him?

He lay down on the cot and closed his eyes. Was he so angry that he was developing psychosomatic symptoms? The light bothered him, and he put the back of one hand over his eyes. He remembered quite a different day that was for ever part of his life tie to Stalin – the one on which all authors were summoned to the Writers' Club to read the secret report that Khrushchev had just delivered to the Twentieth Congress of

CHAPTER 8

the Communist Party.* He could swear that it was possible at one and the same time for the human heart to become as heavy as lead and as light as a puff of dandelion. To read that the human god he had worshipped since childhood had also been a monster who had ordered the imprisonment, the torture and the shooting of millions of innocent citizens was the most painful experience of his life. And yet it was enormously relieving at the same time to have sense made of the many disparate events that had plagued everyone for so many years – the arrests and mysterious disappearances… above all, to believe that it would not, could not ever happen again.

It had not happened again, but still, *he* was now in a cage. And others were in other cages! It was not to be explained away – it was evil! And it was insufferable to yearn to have a child with a woman, but within the same day to become so distrustful of her as to believe she had informed on him. If Lidia indeed was an informer, it was evidence of the way in which a secret police could ensnare, coerce and corrupt people. But if she was honest, the open insinuation that she was an informer could cause him to cruelly wound both her and himself. Either way it was horrid, evil. What a foul day this was in his life!

He felt his forehead. Why was he so hot? He was actually feverish. And his joints were beginning to ache.

He got up and crossed to the door. He hit it twice with his fist. He waited and hit it twice again. Another wait and he struck it three times. The peephole opened. The pale-blue eye looked at him, and the deep voice asked, "What do you want?"

"Some water, please. And I would like a doctor to see me. I'm beginning to feel ill."

"No water, no doctor!" The peephole started to close.

"Wait! What do you mean, 'no water'? What the hell's going on here?"

"Instructions – no water!"

"I demand to see a doctor!"

"You just saw a doctor. She injected you, didn't she?"

THE EYEWITNESS REPORT

"It was to calm my nerves, but I feel—"

The bass voice interrupted with a laugh. "You're beginning to feel feverish, eh? A little weakness? Some aching in your bones? Nothing unusual! Wait until half an hour from now. You will feel like hell, chum – you will feel you're in a deep pit of hell!"

The peephole closed!

Chapter 9

I

His mouth was parched, and his thirst was acute. There was a hot ache in his joints. The strength had so drained from his body that it felt like a lump of soft wax. More threatening than anything else was the fear that if his fever moved higher he would slide into delirium. He wanted to be able to think – to know what was happening to him, however painful it was.

How long had it been since the injection? His sense of time had deserted him. He only knew that each minute was as heavy as lead.

Was the peephole opening? With effort he raised up on an elbow. No – it was his imagination. He fell back on the cot. Dry throat, dry mouth, tongue feeling swollen. How many hours could a man in fever go without water?

He felt so frightfully alone! When he was wounded in the war, he had suffered pain, but not such dreadful loneliness. If only he had Anna beside him so he could touch her hand!

Or if he could occupy his mind with a train of thought! He had been trying, but his brain was becoming increasingly uncontrollable. Thoughts hopped away like fleas.

Out of nowhere came the memory of a winter day when he had gone ice-skating with Ilya. He tried to picture where they had skated. Instead, he saw the pock-marked, beloved face of his father as he lay paralysed after his stroke.

How kind his father had been, what a dedicated Communist! He had learnt from him to believe in the nobility of socialist ideals.

That damn bitch-face kept taunting him!

Nothing would ever shake him from those beliefs, not even...
He wanted to push the bitch-face into that pail of piss.

The socialist dream was a true one! Mankind had conceived of human brotherhood, and therefore it *would* become a reality someday. Even here, in this cage, he would proclaim it!

The bitch-face again! Not everyone was kind. Oh, no!

Yet the first time he was wounded the nurse had been so tender as she changed his bandage, asking if he had a girl – did he want her to write a letter for him, since he had been wounded in the arm?

He seemed to be developing a migraine headache. He never had had one before, but Ilya suffered from them. There were shooting pains in the left side of his head. And his left eye was beginning to blink and trickle tears. Oh, the bastards! They knew how to lacerate a man without leaving bruises on his body.

How unbelievably heavy time was! Why couldn't he think of something interesting to make time pass easier? Like his exciting trip on the fishing fleet out of Murmansk.* If he could recall the series of articles he had written...

Water! He had to have some water! Trembling, he pushed himself upright on the cot. His head swam, the walls turned. He got his legs to the floor. He started to stand and fell back to a sitting position. He waited, breathing heavily, his left eye blurring with tears.

Had they done the same thing to General Grigorenko when they locked him up? He had heard no whispers about it when Grigorenko was released. Or was this a recent inspiration of the KGB – to torture a man with drugs until they broke his spirit and turned him into their creature?

Fuck them!

He got to his feet, staggered, regained balance. Trembling, weaving, he got to the door. He hit it weakly with his fist. He hit it weakly again. Again.

The blue eye was looking at him!

"Water! I must have water!"

CHAPTER 9

The eye disappeared.

He sobbed. Then he shouted weakly, "Fascists, you fascists, screw the whole lot of you!"

He dropped to his knees. He remembered a face – the tortured face of the young girl partisan he had seen hanged in his first days at the front. A round, innocent face with ice on it – frozen short black hair standing upright in the wind, her frozen coat and undergarments deliberately pulled away from her young body so that she would be humiliated before the watching German soldiers, humiliated until her last moment.

Fascists, all of them, no matter the uniform, no matter the white coats!

His arms were trembling so severely that he scarcely could crawl. If Shika were here, they would give each other strength. To be alone was terrible. Was that poor demonstrator alone, the one whose teeth had been kicked out?

He reached the cot, but couldn't raise himself up to it. They had been right – the demonstrators on Red Square had been right to bear witness!

The migraine had become terrible. How heavy a minute was! Interminable! He groaned aloud as he fell at full length on the floor.

Parched mouth... hot joints... a metronome of pain in his head...

Without being aware of it, he began to mutter his thoughts aloud. Was someone in this cage with him? He could hear groaning. Or was he only hearing himself?

He tried to listen. The groaning seemed to be coming from a distance. Who could possibly be with him? He listened again – frightened, yet afraid not to listen.

He began to mumble incoherently as he found the answer. It was TIME that was groaning. They had injected him, and they had injected TIME.

He slipped into unconsciousness.

2

He dreamt that he had been wedged by force into an iron coffin that was too small for his body. For hours he had been achingly uncomfortable. But now suddenly the coffin had begun contracting. The top was pressing down on him, the sides were pressing in, the bottom was pushing mercilessly against his feet. He tried to scream for help, but found that his lips were sewn together by heavy thread. It was agony beyond agony!

He awakened as hands lifted him from the floor onto the cot. An arm around his back raised him. Something cool touched his lips. He went wild as he tasted water. He gulped at it so fiercely that he gagged.

A stern voice said, "Drink slowly!" He opened his eyes. Kulagin was looking at him. Grigory was there with the cup in his hand. Kolya was the one who was holding him up. He realized at once that the effects of the injection had worn off. He felt debilitated, but his brain was clear, and he no longer had aching joints or a headache. He finished drinking the cup of water and cried, "More, I need more, *please.*"

"No more!" Kulagin said intensely. "Now listen to me! You are mentally sick! Your sickness is the way you think! If you don't learn to correct your thinking, you will be sent to a psychiatric hospital. We'll keep you there for life, if necessary. Do you think Barkov the writer can't be turned into Barkov the imbecile? It can be accomplished easily... Turn him over!"

"No!" he protested weakly.

He was turned face down by strong hands. His pyjama bottom was pulled down. A needle stabbed his left buttock.

"Did you enjoy the sulfazin?" Kulagin asked, biting off his words. "You can now compare it with Stelazine.* Let me inform you about Stelazine. It does wonders for schizophrenics, an extremely useful drug. But, of course, the dose must

CHAPTER 9

be regulated. It also has bad side effects, unless prophylactic medicines are administered. I have just given you a heavy dose without prophylactic drugs. Enjoy yourself, you mush-head!"

He heard them walking out. The door closed, the key turned.

Now he felt a fear more disembowelling than the fear of death had been in war: that they *would* turn him mad.

If the safety of his people and his land were at stake, he knew he would put on a soldier's uniform again. He believed he also could endure the hardships of a prison camp – so many had, why not he?

But madness?

"A heavy dose without prophylactic drugs!" And this in the name of correct thinking for the sake of socialist progress. Oh, the foul bastards! What if they continued to give him drug after drug? "Do you think Barkov the writer can't be turned into Barkov the imbecile?"

"Anna," he cried aloud, "Anna." And then, "Shika." And then, "Father."

He began to weep. But not for long. He remembered the bitterly satiric unpublished song by Galich* that he had heard so many times on tape:

> How easy it is to become rich,
> How easy it is to become famous!
> How easy it is to become a hangman!
> Keep quiet! Keep quiet! Keep quiet!

He clenched his teeth and hands and hammered his fists on the cot in a burst of fury. Screw these fascists. He would endure!

3

The dry mouth and thirst had returned. His brain had begun to slow down, to think unfinished, wildly disturbing thoughts. A sense of fear was in each pulse beat. And TIME had taken on a visible shape. TIME was a hyena sitting on his chest, its breath fetid and suffocating.

"Endure!" he told himself. "You have to endure!"

Time passed. Thoughts came and went in random fashion. Gradually he became aware that the muscles of both arms were commencing to feel somewhat stiff and sore. He began to move them, but it was not comfortable to do so: it hurt. He stopped trying.

At last his brain focused on something: the intensely satisfying fantasy that he was killing Kulagin. His fantasy dressed Kulagin in a Nazi uniform, and he began to destroy him in all of the different ways in which he had seen men destroyed in war. He took quick aim with his rifle and shot Kulagin in the throat, the blood from an artery spurting high. He kept his finger on the trigger of his heavy machine gun until Kulagin's intestines spilt out of his belly cavity. He threw a hand grenade and ripped his arms off. He burned him to ash with a flame thrower. But the satisfaction gradually leaked out of the fantasy. He was on a canvas cot in a cage, and the weight of the hyena was heavy on his chest.

And now the right side of his neck was aching. He moved his head from side to side to try and relax his neck, but it did no good. He tried to move his right hand up to rub his neck, but the muscles of his arm were so sore that he let his hand fall back again.

What was happening? It must, he realized, be the effect of the Stelazine. Endure, he told himself forlornly, but the hyena laughed as he felt a sudden stab of pain in his neck. In spite of the soreness of his arm, his hand gripped the right side of his neck. With fright he felt the rigidity of the muscles there and knew they were in spasm. Almost immediately something dreadful began to happen: his head began to be pulled over towards his right shoulder. He fought it, but as the spasm of his neck muscles became more intense, there was nothing he could do about it. Locked in a vice of pain, his head moved

CHAPTER 9

sideways and down until finally his right cheek was touching his right shoulder. There it stayed.

There was fear in his stomach, and fear in his hammering heart, and fear in his veins. "Endure," his mind said weakly.

He gagged as his tongue suddenly flopped back in his mouth. His tongue was choking him, thrusting itself towards his throat. Concentrating on it, willing it, he moved his tongue forward. Almost at once it flopped back again, and this time he could do nothing about it. He gagged and gagged. Spittle ran out of the side of his mouth.

He lay like that, unable to move. With sick fear he heard Kulagin's voice again and again, as though he were in an echo chamber: "Barkov the imbecile…"

4

He had passed through a seemingly endless nightmare of pain and fear, but during it the physical symptoms had begun to diminish. Now he was free of pain. His tongue and his head had returned to their normal positions. He was bothered only by residual muscle soreness in his neck and arms.

But the fear remained, and was overpowering. He didn't need more injections to know that this was a one-sided conflict he could not win. If he wanted to survive as a sane human being, he could only do so by pretending a submission that would get him out of this cage.

He lay inert, breathing shallowly. His body was drained of strength. He wondered what he could say to Kulagin that would make sense and be persuasive. He didn't know.

Time passed – and then they were back again. Kolya lifted him up and Grigory held a cup of water to his lips. Kulagin said, "Drink it slowly," but the advice was not needed. He was too weak to do otherwise. When the cup was withdrawn, Kolya still kept him in a sitting position. Doctor Kulagin held a hypodermic syringe in front of his face. It was partially filled with liquid.

"This is haloperidol.* Did you enjoy the Stelazine? You will enjoy this less. Now, what is it to be? Do you want to go home and behave like a loyal Soviet citizen or do we keep you here?"

Despite himself Barkov answered "Home" with a sob. He had not expected to be offered so easy a way out.

"Go to sleep," Kulagin told him. "We'll see what you say when you awaken. The haloperidol will be waiting!"

The relief Barkov felt was so overwhelming that within the instant he was asleep. His exhaustion was more emotional than physical, and he slept for almost twenty hours. Three times during that period he was awakened – given a cup of water and fed buckwheat porridge and milk – yet his sleep was so deep that when a hand on his shoulder finally shook him fully awake, he had no memory of the feedings. He saw a new orderly.

"I am Leonid. Doctor Kulagin wants to see you. I've brought you something to eat. Sit up."

With instant recollection of everything that had preceded his sleep, Barkov obeyed. Although the muscles of his arms and neck still were sore, he felt refreshed and otherwise normal.

Leonid placed a tray on his thighs. There was tea, two thick slices of buttered pumpernickel, an omelette. He dropped the two lumps of sugar into the tea and began to eat hungrily. In between mouthfuls he asked, "What day is it, please?"

"Thursday." Leonid's voice had gravel in it. His bulk and short, up-turned nose made Barkov, with distaste, remember Snub-Nose on Red Square.

"And what time of day?"

"Four thirty in the afternoon."

He shivered inwardly at the realization that three full days had passed since Doctor Larina had given him the first injection. They had warned him that they would not allow him to join the ranks of the open dissenters, and this they certainly had achieved! Yet, as he thought about it, his surrender was only a partial victory for them. Since they wanted him to be a member of the orthodox literary establishment, they had to set him free. Once free, he no longer was helpless. How he would conduct himself depended upon two factors: the conditions they would attach to his release – and his own ingenuity. He had to learn what the first were before he could make use of the second.

He was not kept waiting long. Within a few minutes after Leonid took the tray out of the room, the door key clicked again and Doctor Kulagin entered. His piercing blue eyes fixed upon Barkov in a look of enquiry and appraisal. Barkov returned a bland glance in spite of his raging hatred for the man.

"Are you clear-headed?"

Barkov nodded.

"Then pay close attention!" Kulagin held out a clipboard with typewritten pages on it. "I have three copies of a statement. If you sign them, you can go home. If you do not, by tomorrow night you will be an inmate of the psychiatric hospital in Oryol. Do you know what life there will be like – do you remember what Kolya told you?"

Barkov nodded. Kolya had called it a prison, but Kulagin, he noted, preferred the fiction of the word "hospital".

"Your commitment there will be followed by a letter from the Ministry of Health to the Writers' Union. The letter will explain that you attempted suicide in despondence over the terminal illness of your wife. In view of your severe depression, you are receiving inpatient treatment. No prognosis for your recovery can be made at this time."

Too much already had been done to Barkov for him to be shocked by this new turn. Nevertheless, he was startled by the finesse with which they had prepared his burial. A communication like that would be accepted readily by the public. It even would be accepted by friends, who knew of his devotion to Anna but had not seen him recently. A single bulletin a year could keep him in Oryol for ever. Anna was the only one who would know with certainty that he was not in a state of depression and that he would not, in any case, have been ready to desert her by committing suicide. But Anna was a helpless invalid: there would be nothing she could do from her hospital bed to combat an official pronouncement by the Ministry of Health.

"This is the statement you will sign," Kulagin continued. He handed him the clipboard. "Read it aloud to me. If you have any questions, put them to me immediately. If you want any statement rephrased, ask me if it is permissible. If you decide not to sign, stop reading and tell me so."

Barkov's eyes took in the first sentences. "Aloud!" Kulagin reminded him sharply. He began to read in a controlled monotone.

29th August 1968

I, Daniil Barkov, voluntarily state the following: after several weeks of emotional and mental distress during which I could not sleep and found myself having fantasies that I recognized to be abnormal, I went to Psychiatric Hospital Number Three in Moscow and asked for medical assistance. I was examined by a commission of psychiatrists consisting of Doctor Dmitry Kulagin, Doctor Raisa Larina and Doctor Boris Rubin. I accepted—

He paused involuntarily as his eyes caught what came next.
"Well?" Kulagin asked. "Any objections?"
Barkov shook his head.

I accepted the diagnosis of this commission that I was suffering from schizophrenia with delusions of grandeur and symptoms of paranoia. I readily agreed to become an inpatient. I am glad to state that as a result of some days of intensive treatment, this same commission has informed me that a remission has taken place in my disease!

CHAPTER 9

He paused momentarily in order to take a deep breath, but then continued in his controlled monotone.

> It has been explained to me that my basic illness is incurable, and that only time will tell if I will remain in a state of remission or if I will again require inpatient treatment. In the mean time, while being allowed to go home and resume my normal life, I agree to return to the hospital at nine o'clock every Tuesday morning for examination and further therapy.

He stopped reading and stared at the paper. With rage and anguish he told himself that it was *his* face that was being thrust into the pail of piss. Nevertheless, he was getting out of this cage. And whatever *they* thought, he never would become their servant.

"Well, will you sign it or not?"

Barkov looked up. "Yes."

"Then sign all three copies – the first for the Ministry of Health, the second for the KGB, the third for this hospital."

He was astonished that his hand remained steady as he signed. Doctor Kulagin took the clipboard with an obvious smile of satisfaction. Then he unfolded a sheet of paper he had taken from the pocket of his white gown. "Now I have some instructions for you. If you violate any one of them, I assure you it won't be long before the KGB learns of it. A single violation will be a sign that you require inpatient treatment for an indefinite period. Clear?"

"Yes."

"First: you are not to tell *anyone* what happened in your three days in this hospital. I will advise you in a moment what you can say to your wife."

Barkov nodded. He had anticipated this.

"Second: you are forbidden to have any uncensored writings in your possession."

THE EYEWITNESS REPORT

"In that case, my home in Peredelkino must be exempt until—"

"It's already been searched. All uncensored manuscripts have been removed. If any are found when it is searched again, you will be responsible."

Barkov nodded.

"Third: you are forbidden from now on to communicate in any way with the Pole Shika Botwin."

"I understand," Barkov murmured, and told himself that he still would find someone trustworthy to carry a message to Shika.

"Fourth: you will write a letter to Ilya Krasny ending your relationship with him. You will tell him that you have come to believe that the Human Rights Committee is anti-Soviet. You will send a copy of the letter to me."

Barkov nodded his acquiescence. Since his letter would reach Ilya so soon after their conversation of Monday, Ilya would be certain to guess that some sort of pressure had been put on him. Sometime in the future he would find a way to tell Ilya more.

"Fifth: you are forbidden to attend, or to observe, any demonstration critical of the government like the one on Red Square on Sunday, or the one on Constitution Day."

He nodded again.

"Sixth: you are forbidden to make any statement orally or in writing critical of the Party's position on any subject. Seventh, you are forbidden to show anything you write to anyone, except your wife, until it first has been read and approved by the psychiatrist with whom you meet weekly. Are these instructions clear?"

"Yes, quite clear," Barkov answered quietly. He now had his answer: he could function in the future only as a member of the literary underground. It was, however, a vital and viable way.

"You are free to go to your home in Peredelkino at any time, provided you see a physician there whom I will assign to you. You may not go anywhere else without written permission from someone on my staff."

CHAPTER 9

"I understand."

"I am aware of the condition of your wife," Kulagin added in a less severe tone. "A daily call was made to her hospital to say that you had sprained your back slightly in a fall and were in the orthopaedic hospital for heat therapy and observation." He paused for a moment. "Since we both know that your wife's illness is terminal, I suggest that you begin to develop your excellent idea for a documentary on the Vietnam War. It will be wholesome therapy for you to undertake such a project." He started out, but paused. "I forgot to mention the unfinished manuscript of your novel, *The Foundryman*."

Barkov caught his breath.

"Since I am taking a personal interest in your case, I have started reading it. The first two chapters are excellent. If no elements of pathology appear in it, the manuscript will be returned to you." He paused once more as he opened the door. "Oh, yes, you will be driven home after you have shaved and showered."

"If no elements of pathology appear in it!..." Barkov reflected calmly that Kulagin's decision about his novel would be final – there would be no opportunity to discuss or argue as one could with a censor. Very well, then! If it was not returned to him, he never would find out if readers and critics agreed that he had grown as a novelist. But from now on he *would* learn something else: whether he was a man of conscience and courage like his father. In the course of a few days, this had become more important to his self-esteem than his achievements as a novelist. He had debased himself in order to stay sane, but not in order to become a tool of the KGB. On Sunday he had enlisted in a war. The fact that he had been trapped in an ambush didn't mean that the war itself was not going on or that he could not participate in it. He would be under surveillance, but he would find the ways to manoeuvre. From now on there could be no other enduring, central objective in his life.

Yet he also had an immediate objective: to learn the truth about Lidia. Kulagin had equivocated on purpose. He had not said that Lidia was an informer for the KGB: he had left it dangling in mid-air. She was too precious for him to reach a conclusion about her based upon a deliberately unclear statement. There had to be some way in which he could discover how the KGB knew what he had told her on Sunday night.

The door to his cage opened, and a smiling Kolya appeared. "You're going home, eh? Congratulations."

"Thank you." He did not add what came to his tongue: "You actually relish the role of a smooth-talking Judas, don't you? Some day, my lad, I'm going to write about you."

"Come on, let's go."

As he stood up and walked out of the room, his mind swerved back to Lidia. He knew what his first step should be: to search his own apartment. If he found microphones there, why, wouldn't it be likely that bugs had been placed in Lidia's apartment without *her* knowledge just as it had been done without his? He could search her apartment thoroughly while she was away at work.

When he entered the room in which he had undressed on Monday, he felt comparatively light-hearted for the first time in the three longest days of his life.

Chapter 10

1

The KGB agent who drove the Volga was a stocky, taciturn man of about thirty. Barkov, sitting in the rear, was glad not to talk. He pulled back the curtains on the side window and peered out. The streets were crowded with trucks, buses and trolleys, the sidewalks with people returning from work or queuing up in front of shops. All along the skyline cranes loomed high over apartment and office buildings under construction. It was good for him to see this. Stalin's ghost lay wickedly heavy on the Soviet Union, but it still was a country that graduated more engineers each year than any other in the world, a land where no one went hungry and no one who was ill went unattended. How many nations were there without their own evils – different, perhaps, but evil nonetheless?

He would begin writing two books immediately. The first would be a short novel called *Anna* – the tale of their meeting while digging an anti-tank trench outside of Moscow. They both had been sixteen, and they had fallen in love that first day. It would be the story of their first year together before he joined the army. It would please Anna so much to have him start it at once. And since it would be published, it would be dust in the eyes of the KGB. The other would be not actually a book, but an endless series of anonymous pamphlets for which he would do steady research. On the one hand he would point out the discrepancies between Marxist theory and Soviet practice in the critical area of human rights. On the other he would demonstrate how these discrepancies, together with the frozen bureaucracy, the secret-police power and the lack of genuine democracy, retarded the growth and impaired the health of the socialist system itself. It would require extreme caution to do this without being caught. A week ago he never would have chosen to make this his life's task. Now he could not avoid it.

It had crossed his mind that there was another path to follow. If Solzhenitsyn were in his situation, he would write an "Open Letter" to the Central Committee of the Party. He would state exactly what had been done to him and denounce everyone concerned by name. He then would get copies of his letter to foreign journalists. But in order to challenge the KGB openly like that he would need Solzhenitsyn's international reputation and Solzhenitsyn's iron will. He didn't have the first, and he doubted that he had the second. The only way *he* could work was underground.

Yet what if the KGB discovered what he was doing? Undoubtedly it would mean a psychiatric prison without the right of appeal to a court. A shudder went through him, but he shook his head and told himself that even to contemplate it would be to paralyse himself. He would have to regain the frame of mind he had had as a soldier, when psychological survival depended upon the belief that one would come through a battle unscathed. Without that, a man went to pieces from anxiety alone.

His thoughts went to his wife. How would he handle things with her if Kulagin did not return the manuscript of *The Foundryman*? He longed to be able to tell her the truth, but it would be far too harrowing for her. Of more immediate concern was to explain why he had decided not to write his 'Eyewitness Report'. He would have to invent a reason by tomorrow morning – she surely would ask about it.

When the auto stopped in front of his apartment house, the driver turned around. He took a small notebook from his pocket and read from it in a matter-of-fact manner. "You will find the following items on the sofa in your apartment: the manuscript of a book your wife has translated; two albums of personal photographs; an unfinished short story of yours entitled 'The Central Committee Member'; your Medal of Valour and the medals of your Stalin and Lenin prizes; your two typewriters, which were found not to have been used in the typing of any self-published manuscripts. Nothing else that was removed will be returned to you. That's all. You can go."

As Barkov walked up the stairs to the second floor, he tried to tick off the items that had not been returned. The five pages of his 'Eyewitness Report', naturally. The two teeth of poor Fainberg. (What was happening to him?) And Shika's letter, damn them. What else? Yes, a number of self-published manuscripts: *The First Circle*; Sakharov's *Progress, Coexistence and Intellectual Freedom*; and the first two issues of *A Chronicle of Current Events*. His lips curled as he recalled several other items: the print by Picasso and a painting by Nasedkin. How miserably petty these bigots were!

In his mailbox there was an unstamped envelope with his name on it. The handwriting was only vaguely familiar. He put it in his pocket, opened the padlocks and took them into his apartment. He went into the kitchen and reached for a bottle of Courvoisier in a cupboard. He poured himself a small drink. Glass in hand, he went into his living room. The typewriters and the other items were on the sofa. He sat down at his desk and dialled the Academy of Sciences Hospital. The night operator, whom he knew by name, told him that his wife's condition was stable. He asked her, please, to get a message to Anna before she fell asleep: that he would visit her at nine in the morning. The operator assured him she would do so.

Rubbing the sore muscles on the right side of his neck, he sniffed the cognac and took a sip of it. Then he noticed the empty spot on the wall where the photograph of Solzhenitsyn had been hanging. A dismaying thought came. What if the rumours became reality and the Stalinist wing in the Writers' Union actually moved to expel Solzhenitsyn?* Expulsion would mean that nothing he wrote in the future would be published.

When it was presented for discussion and a vote, what position would *he* take? There could be no doubt that Kulagin would be in touch with him in advance about a matter of such importance. He certainly would not be permitted to defend Solzhenitsyn in the debate. Since he would not attack him or vote for expulsion at any cost to himself, he could propose a compromise to Kulagin: that he become ill and not go to the meeting. It was likely that the KGB would accept that. It would be enough for their purpose if he kept quiet.

Barkov sighed and drank off his cognac. A certain amount of humiliation would be part of his spiritual diet for the rest of his life. There would be more than one occasion in the future when they would shove his head into their pail of piss.

He took the envelope out of his pocket. The moment he saw the signature – Lidia – he became very tense. The letter was an agitated one. It expressed deep bewilderment, sharp reproach and entreaty. When he hadn't met her in the lobby of the Ukraina on Monday evening, she had kept calling his apartment. Finally, frightened, she had telephoned the Academy of Sciences Hospital. Using a false name, she stated that she worked for *Novy Mir* and had an appointment with him which he had failed to keep. She asked the telephone operator to enquire about him from his wife. In that way she learnt about his fall and the fact that he was in a hospital. But why hadn't he telephoned her or asked someone else to convey a message? It was utterly mystifying, and she was distraught with worry. Would he *please* call her at work or at home the moment he read this?

The letter seemed to have been written with such deep sincerity that he automatically reached for the telephone. This was the loving, passionate Lidia he knew. No informer for the KGB could have written a letter with so many cross-currents of true emotion.

His intellect pulled him back at once from this hasty conclusion. He only had to remind himself that for years Lenin

CHAPTER 10

had had a close, trusted friend who later was revealed to be a tsarist police agent. There were innumerable such examples. He needed more evidence than this to regain confidence in her.

He stood up and looked around the room. If there were microphones in his apartment, where would they be? He had no experience at this sort of thing, but everyone had heard whispered talk. Light fixtures were one place in which bugs were said to be placed. And the mouthpiece of the telephone. Where else? He couldn't remember. The only thing he could do was to scan each room as alertly as he could. He would assume that a microphone needed to be attached to a wire that ran to a listening post or a tape recorder.

He unscrewed the mouthpiece of his telephone and saw nothing meaningful. For all he knew, the mechanism inside could function both as a microphone and as a normal telephone. When he had examined everything he could think of in the living room, he moved into the bedroom. A few minutes later he was startled by a loud knocking on his door. For an instant he panicked. Had *they* returned?

He decided it was someone else. Lidia? No, she would have telephoned.

The knocking was repeated. He went to the door and called hoarsely, "Who is it?"

"Sandler."

He opened the door and took a step forward so that his broad shoulders filled the doorway and Sandler could not enter. Sandler had been smiling, but a puzzled look came to his face as Barkov did this. He said in a whisper, "I suppose you've been down at Peredelkino? I was here last night and the night before." He lifted his portfolio. "I have some items for you. One is very exciting."

"Listen to me," Barkov told him harshly, but keeping his voice low, "this is where you and I part company. After what those damn Czechs tried to do, and after that anti-Soviet demonstration by those hooligans on Sunday, I'll have nothing more to do with you or your kind. This isn't why I shed my blood in the war. If you ever approach me again, I'll report you to the KGB."

He stepped back and slammed the door. It seemed to him that he could feel Sandler's heart beating on the other side of the door, beating with confusion and dismay. Then he heard quick footsteps moving off.

How degrading! But there would be one result of it that was useful: Sandler would report it to Ilya at once – and Ilya would get the message.

He returned to the bedroom. Neither there nor in the kitchen could he find anything, but this didn't prove that his apartment was free of bugs. It might only mean that he was not sufficiently trained to find them. Or perhaps there was a listening device in a neighbour's apartment. He had heard whispers of that type of contrivance more than once: a microphone pressed to a wall and attached to an automatic tape recorder. He only had a superficial acquaintance with his neighbours. If they had been approached some time ago by the KGB and asked to cooperate, they certainly would have done so without telling him.

And Lidia? Hopefully he would find microphones in her apartment, but no search was possible before she went to work in the morning. In the mean time he needed to see her. He wanted to look into her eyes, to hear the tone of her voice, to touch her with the antenna of his inner heart.

He went to the telephone, breathed deeply, and dialled her number. After the phone had rung several times he looked at his watch. It was seven thirty-five. Normally she was finished with supper by that hour. But it was possible that she might be attending an evening meeting at the Institute. If so...

When he heard her voice and said "Lidia, I'm home", her cry of relief – "Thank God, I was afraid you were dead" – moved him deeply. He asked if he could come right over to see her.

"*If...*" she replied intensely. "How ridiculous! You *must* come. Don't waste time walking. Take a taxi, *please*."

He said he would if he could find one.

CHAPTER 10

2

The rear of the Hotel Ukraina was just across the Kutuzovsky Prospect from his apartment house. As he crossed the wide avenue and circled the massive hotel, several things Lidia had said on Sunday night came to mind. They had great relevance now. She had warned that if he put his name on his 'Eyewitness Report', it would prevent Shika from being granted a Soviet visa. Would a KGB informer react spontaneously with advice like that? It wouldn't seem so. And something else: she had offered him the use of her new typewriter if he used a pseudonym. In that way the manuscript could not be traced to his typewriter.

These recollections excited him and made him happy momentarily, but his good cheer did not last long. Logic warned that he was being sentimental again. These were only presumptive pieces of evidence, not conclusive ones. Why, wasn't it equally possible that she had said those things in order to ingratiate herself with him?

A new, extremely disturbing thought came: was it possible that when she first arrived at the hospital with a bouquet of flowers in her hand, she had done so on instructions from the KGB? He groaned aloud – he felt as though he had been struck a blow. It never had occurred to him before that there actually was something odd about her having appeared at the hospital *when Anna was in a coma*. The ostensible reason for her coming was to convey the sympathy and best wishes of Anna's fellow workers at the Institute. But why hadn't she telephoned to find out if Anna could receive visitors? It was the normal, natural thing to do.

Yet how could she have known that *he* was at the hospital? The answer came instantly: from the KGB. They would have told her that he left the hospital only to eat and sleep. He groaned aloud again. It seemed all too possible now that she had come to see *him*, not Anna.

He suddenly shook his head and told himself to stop thinking. These conjectures were turning him away from Lidia before he even set eyes on her. He needed to wait, and not leap to conclusions.

There was no taxi in front of the Ukraina. He stood for half a minute massaging the sore muscles of both upper arms. He decided to walk – it was only ten minutes to her apartment. He had just started off when he saw a taxi approaching. He turned back and ran to meet it. He knew the chauffeur, a woman in her late fifties who had driven him before. The moment her passengers – three tall Africans in native dress – got out, he called to her. "Comrade Paridova, good evening – are you free to take me?"

"Ah, it's you, eh? But I was just going to end my day. How far are you going?"

"Only a kilometre."

"Get in."

He sat down beside her in the front. She was a stout, grey-haired, cheerful-looking woman. She offered him a cigarette as they started off, and then said, "I forgot, you don't smoke. How is your poor wife?"

"I expect to be taking her home in about ten days. How have you been?"

"Today I'm very happy." Her big smile revealed strong, tobacco-stained teeth. "I heard from my Tanya. She's such a bad letter writer I'd like to strap her behind."

"Where is she?"

"Don't you remember? In the Urals. I told you she was—"

"Oh yes, the geologist," he interrupted. "I remember very well. How is she getting along?"

With great pride the mother began to talk about her smart little one, who was a member of an expedition looking for minerals, but Barkov's mind drifted to Lidia, and he didn't listen. What would he learn when he searched her apartment tomorrow morning? Nothing! Even if he found microphones,

CHAPTER 10

he still could not be certain that Lidia herself had not informed on him. It was well known that the KGB distrusted its own creatures and constantly double-checked them. The microphones could be there with or without her knowledge, and there was no way in which he ever could find out. Furthermore, why was it that he had not been questioned about anything he and Anna had discussed in their apartment? Kulagin had quoted only what he said to Lidia. Why?

On the other hand, why was it that Lidia never had tried to draw him out on political matters? Surely that would be a natural thing for an informer to do? On Sunday night it was he who had started the political talk, not she.

"Hey there," the mother said loudly, "why don't you answer?"

"I'm sorry, something popped into my head. What was it you asked?"

"I said that when I was born in the time of the tsar, there were chickens, bedbugs and lice in the same dirty little hut. What working woman at that time voted, or got a paid vacation, or had a daughter who went to the university and became a geologist? Isn't it a miracle?"

"A miracle indeed!"

"Still and all, I haven't given up my religion. The government is atheist, but I'm a believer. Of course, I don't go to church, because I might lose the right to be a chauffeur. Say..." – she looked at him with sudden apprehension – "you're not a tattle-tale, are you?"

"Don't worry, comrade."

"No, of course you're not, I apologize for even asking. But a person has to be careful. It was that way under the tsar – it's the same now. Do as you're told and you get along fine. But act snotty and look out! That never changes, does it?"

"It doesn't seem to," he muttered, and thought to himself bitterly that the coincidence of being told this by a taxi driver on this particular night was almost a mathematical impossibility.

3

He felt nervous and increasingly unhappy as the elevator took him up to Lidia's floor. The very purpose of his visit was debasing to both of them. When he knocked, she opened the door immediately with a low cry of "Daniil, Daniil!" – but it was not the unalloyed exclamation of happiness that he somehow had expected. Her eyes were searching as well as glad, and although she embraced him and offered her lips, she pulled away rather quickly and stared at him again in a searching manner. "Come in, we need to talk," she said hurriedly in a flustered way. For reasons that had nothing to do with logic, he was distressed by the fact that she was dressed in the same blouse and skirt she had worn on her first visit to the hospital.

On the table in her living room were two glasses and the second bottle of cognac he had brought with him on Sunday night.

"Will you pour a little for me?" It was obvious that she was nervous. She was lighting a cigarette with trembling hands.

He did so and sat down beside her on the sofa.

"Aren't you going to drink?"

"Not at the moment."

"I don't understand your behaviour towards me," she burst out abruptly and emotionally. "I simply don't understand it. There's no use my pretending everything is as usual between us, because it isn't."

"My behaviour? What do you mean?" He knew from her letter what she would answer, but there was a need to play this chess game slowly, move by move, while he studied her. He already was grateful for the intensity of her reproach. It felt true.

"What do I mean?" Her dark eyes blazed, and her hand cut the air in a nervous, spastic gesture. "On Monday you had a fall and were taken to the orthopaedic hospital. Did a sprained back make you forget that you had an appointment to meet me?"

He gave her the answer he had prepared. "My back muscles went into spasm, Lidia. I was given an injection and I didn't awaken until Tuesday morning."

CHAPTER 10

"But this is Thursday night. Why didn't you have a nurse call me on Tuesday?"

"I did."

"No one called me."

"That's incredible!" he exclaimed smoothly. "The nurse told me she reached you at the Institute and spoke to you."

"No one from the hospital spoke to me, no one!"

"Then that explains why you didn't come to visit me."

Lidia jumped up with unconcealed exasperation. "Why didn't you have someone call me again?"

"Until this morning I was kept under mild sedation so my muscles would relax. I slept most of the time I was there and most of today as well."

"You're lying, you're lying, you're lying!" Lidia screamed. "I *went* to the hospital. You weren't on the list of patients. You didn't have a fall, you didn't sprain your back. You've been away four days with another woman!" She hid her face in her hands and burst into sobs of such deep anguish that her whole body shook.

Barkov's heart began to pound. What she had charged him with was so unexpected that it felt all the more true. And her emotion felt true – he couldn't believe she was contriving it. He stood up and took hold of her arms. "Listen to me. I was *not* with another woman. If I had been, wouldn't it have been simple for me to telephone you with an excuse?"

Her hands jerked away nervously from her distraught face, which was wet with tears. "Don't tell me again that you were in the hospital – don't dare!"

"That's right, I was not. It was a story for Anna so she wouldn't worry."

"Then where were you?"

He said the first thing that came to his mind. "Away from Moscow."

"Where?"

"I can't tell you where or why."

"Why can't you tell me? This is bewildering."

171

"I'm sorry, but there's no use your asking me."

"But why didn't you at least telephone me? You let me wait at the Ukraina worried sick that you'd been—"

He interrupted quickly. "No telephone was available to me."

"That's ridiculous! How could you be any place where no telephone…" She stopped with her mouth open and stared at him. "My God," she exclaimed. "Were you photographed at the demonstration on Sunday? Is that where you've been for four days – under arrest for interrogation?"

"Oh, no," he responded at once. "What gave you an idea like that?"

"You said no telephone was available to you, but you weren't hunting in the forests of Siberia. How can I believe that for four days you couldn't reach a telephone in order to tell me you were all right? Don't you realize the awful choice you gave me? When I found that you weren't at the hospital, I either had to believe you were mysteriously dead – it can happen – or else that you had taken up with another woman."

"If I had, why would I be here now?"

"I don't know. I'm hurt and completely confused."

He stared at her. Would an informer carry on like this? It wouldn't seem so. Unless she had been instructed to do it and was a natural actress. He couldn't forget the police agent who had been Lenin's co-worker and friend.

Lidia suddenly caught her breath in a sob and burst out forlornly and bitterly: "You're not a woman of my generation with half the men of her age group dead and a good many of the others happy to be womanizers. You haven't been lied to and toyed with. You haven't had your need for love abused again and again."

With sudden pity Barkov put his arms around her. "I cherish you, Lidia. That's why I'm here now – it's the only reason."

"Then look into my heart for just one moment. I'm at a point in my life where I must be able to trust a man, or there can't be anything good between us. What would you be feeling now if

CHAPTER 10

you were in my place? Wouldn't you want to know more than you've told me? Don't you see that I need a better explanation than you've given me?"

His embrace slackened. Why this persistence? Was it truly an inner need or was it guile? Kulagin's first instruction had been that he must not tell *anyone* what had happened in the four days. Had Lidia been instructed to test him, to wheedle it out of him if she could? Why in the Devil's name had she chosen to wear the identical skirt and blouse with which she first appeared at the hospital? And why *had* she come when Anna was in a coma?

"Yes," he answered mechanically, "in your place I might want to know more. But I can't tell you any more. It was something personal, but it was not another woman."

Lidia sighed deeply. Her eyes locked on his as she wiped her cheeks with her hand. After a while she said, very slowly, "I suppose... there's nothing to do except... try to trust you." Suddenly she flung her arms around his neck and pressed her body against his. "Oh, Daniil!" She kissed him feverishly. He met her kiss, wanting to reassure her, yet at the same time wondering with unease why a woman who had been exploited by men and resented it bitterly could – as she was doing now – shift so quickly into seeking comfort and reassurance in sexuality.

Her mouth had locked on his, her tongue sought his, one hand grasped his and moved it to her breast. He fondled and caressed her and met her kiss for kiss, and then became aware that he was not responding. He opened the buttons of her blouse so that he could feel her warm flesh. She was not wearing a brassiere (why not?), and when his hand cupped her breast, whose loveliness he saw in his mind's eye, there still was no stirring of his senses. It was incredible. This was a woman who had made him flame from the first time she kissed him.

The answer came, and he knew there was no way to evade its sour truth. In spite of her emotion, her anger, her tears, he could not trust her. Kulagin, and his own suspicions, had poisoned him. To love her, to even respond to her sexually, he had to know absolutely that she was not an informer – but there was no way he ever could know it with certainty.

He moved away from her. She looked at him with surprise and distress. "What's wrong?"

His answer was cold. "I don't seem to be very amorous tonight."

Her fingers trembled as she buttoned her blouse. Her voice was trembling also when she finally spoke. "Now I know you were with another woman. Just go."

He went towards the door with the thought that if she were honest (and he never would be sure), it was better this way than if he had invented some flabby excuse to break with her. Her anger towards him would help her. At the door he was sorry to hear her cry out "Don't go, Daniil, let's talk", because it poisoned him even more. He left without looking back.

4

The telephone was ringing when he opened the door to his apartment. Lidia, he thought, and did not answer it. He poured half a glass of cognac and drained it quickly. The ringing stopped. He poured again. He didn't intend to get drunk, but he needed some help in easing the ache in his heart. If she *was* an informer, it was a revolting example of the manner in which a secret police corrupted and made use of otherwise decent people. But if she was *not*, then he had inflicted terrible and needless pain upon himself, and upon an innocent, lonely woman he had come to cherish. Yet he could do nothing else, and in this the bastards had triumphed quite completely.

He drank off the glass and put it down. He went to his desk and stared at the yellow pad. How could he write an anonymous work without being caught? How could he throw hot lead in their teeth without their tracing the manuscript to him?

The simplest of the problems was the final typing. He could buy a new typewriter each year. A bit expensive, but safe so long as he bought them in different department or foreign-currency

CHAPTER 10

stores. He would type several copies of a year's work on the new typewriter, then smash the type with a hammer and throw the machine into the river! There would be no way ever of tracing the manuscripts to him.

Much harder was hiding the manuscript while he was writing it by hand. The KGB would make periodic searches of his apartment and country home. In the apartment he would only be able to do a little writing. He could hide half a dozen sheets of paper in different books on his shelves and be fairly certain they wouldn't search all of his books thoroughly enough to find them. And especially so because on his desk would be the growing manuscript called *Anna*. The main part of his underground writing would have to be done at Peredelkino. The house there had advantages. When he sat at his desk, he looked out at the lane that ran from the road to his front door. He always would know in advance if anyone were coming. He also could buy a watchdog, so that if he were elsewhere in the house, he would be alerted by barking.

But how could he handle his manuscript as it grew in size? A recess under a floorboard? They were too likely to be alert to that possibility. What else?

His woodpile! His neighbours knew that he chopped wood for exercise and to feed the fireplace. The thick hedge around the yard hid him from view, but the sound of his axe could be heard. Therefore, there was nothing unusual about his presence in the yard at any season of the year or at any hour. He could saw one or several logs in half and partially hollow them out. Then he could carve their severed ends for a tongue-and-groove fitting as carpenters do. Since he always had a good-sized woodpile, he could slip them in here and there.

Or maybe he would find a better way to hide his manuscript when he was down there and studied the opportunities. The thick legs of his kitchen table, perhaps, or a sliding panel in the eaves. Without doubt it could be solved! Over fifty years ago his father had become an illegal member of the underground while serving in the tsar's army. Why couldn't his son also? True, his father had not had the burden of being alone. (Oh, Anna, he thought, how deeply I need you now!) But the day he mailed copies of his first manuscripts to Sandler and to several other members of the Human Rights Committee would be the day he no longer felt absolutely alone. They would see to it that his ideas began to circulate throughout the land.

He picked up a pen. He had to begin now, he couldn't wait. He knew what the title would be

Humanity Is in a Cage
by
Anonymous

– but he would not write it now. It would be the very last page he wrote. He began:

"I am a man of middle years in the last third of the twentieth century. How does it go with me?"

The phone rang. Lidia, he thought with a pang of terrible sorrow. He listened to it ring, then locked his teeth and resumed writing.

"It does not go well!"

"How does it go with mankind? Not at all well! Not anywhere!"

The phone was still ringing.

"For one reason or another, or for many reasons, every person on earth lives in a cage."

The ringing stopped.

"There is only one solution: to oppose that which is indecent, unjust and wrong and to strive for that which is human, just and right. It is a struggle that will take many forms, but it is the only possible solution to the human condition."

He continued writing.

Notes

p. 1, *The Eyewitness Report*: Maltz's original title for *The Eyewitness Report* was 'The Cage', taken from the famous pantomime narrative of that title by Marcel Marceau (1923–2007). Maltz toyed with the idea of using an image of Marceau in performance as the cover of the novel. The meaning is addressed in the text as Barkov realizes that "all of mankind lived in one sort of cage or another". Maltz knew Marceau personally, and they corresponded while the book was in progress. In a letter to Marceau dated 27th December 1972, he informed the Frenchman that he had been "working all year" on the novel and was "deeply excited by the materials".

p. 1, *Many mistakes... verity!*: This epigraph is taken from Book One of *Dead Souls*, an 1842 novel by Nikolai Gogol (1809–52). The translation quoted by Maltz is by Constance Garnett (1861–1946). Maltz used a longer version of the same epigraph in his novel *The Cross and the Arrow* (1944).

p. 3, *my wife, Esther*: Esther Engelberg (née Goldstein, 1913–98), Maltz's third wife, whom he married in 1970. Her first marriage was to Doctor Hyman Engelberg (1913–2005), who was the personal physician of Marilyn Monroe (1926–62). She was born in New York and died in Los Angeles.

p. 5, *B.K.R.*: The recipient of this acknowledgement cannot be traced among the Red Square demonstrators or other dissidents, and might be fictitious. No name can be found in Maltz's notes, letters or journals that fits these initials. Maltz may have inserted a fake acknowledgement to a Soviet "eyewitness" because he was having trouble getting publishers to take on a novel about the USSR by an American writer. Correspondence between Maltz and his literary agent Roslyn Targ indicates that at least once the manuscript was submitted under the name "Yuri Krasnov".

THE EYEWITNESS REPORT

- p. 7, *25th August 1968*: For the events of 25th August 1968 narrated in this chapter, Maltz drew from first-hand sources quoted in the first chapter of *Red Square at Noon* by Natalya Gorbanevskaya (see first note to p. 13), published in the UK by André Deutsch and in the USA by Holt, Rinehart and Winston in 1972 (tr. Alexander Lieven), pp. 27–41 (Holt edn). These include an 'Eye-Witness Account of the Demonstration', 'What I [Natalya Gorbanevskaya] Remember of the Demonstration' and 'The Account of Tania Baeva, the Eighth Participant in the Demonstration' (see fourth note to p. 13).
- p. 7, *the ancient monument called "Execution Ground"*: The monument in question, known as Lobnoye Mesto – a name meaning literally "Forehead Place", and that is sometimes translated as "Place of the Skull" – is a thirteen-metre-long circular stone platform in front of Saint Basil's Cathedral in Red Square. Dating from the early sixteenth century, it was principally used by the tsar and other official figures to make announcements and promulgate decrees. It is traditionally believed to have been a place of execution, although in fact there is no evidence that it was ever used for this purpose.
- p. 10, *Pravda*: At the time in which the novel is set, the official newspaper of the Central Committee of the Communist Party of the Soviet Union.
- p. 10, *St George*: The patron saint of Moscow.
- p. 12, *Pavel Litvinov*: The Russian-born US physicist and human-rights activist Pavel Litvinov (born 1940), the grandson of the Russian revolutionary and Soviet statesman Maxim Litvinov (1876–1951).
- p. 13, *The young, round-faced mother*: The Russian civil-rights activist, poet and translator Natalya Gorbanevskaya (1936–2013).
- p. 13, *a smiling woman... the oldest of the group, about forty*: The Russian dissident Larisa Bogoraz (1929–2004), then married to the imprisoned writer Yuli Daniel (1925–88).

NOTES

p. 13, *a young, slender man*: The Russian poet and dissident Vadim Delaunay (1947–83).

p. 13, *an attractive girl who looked like a student*: Tatyana Baeva (born 1947).

p. 13, *a tall man in his late twenties*: The Soviet dissident Vladimir Dremlyuga (1940–2015).

p. 13, *two more men, both approaching forty*: Respectively, the Russian philologist Viktor Fainberg (1931–2023) and the Russian linguist Konstantin Babitsky (1929–93).

p. 14, *Was this... Black Hundreds*: The "Black Hundreds" were groups of reactionary, anti-Semitic extremists who supported the tsar. In 1908, Lenin, chased by the tsarist police, was forced to flee Russia and return to exile in Switzerland.

p. 17, *American Embassy to protest the murder of the Vietnamese*: The novel is set at the height of the Vietnam War (1955–75), a conflict between the guerrilla fighters of North Vietnam ("Viet Cong", supported by the Soviet Union) and the forces of South Vietnam (supported by America and other anti-communist countries).

p. 18, *Izvestia*: At the time in which the novel is set, the organ of the Supreme Soviet of the Soviet Union.

p. 19, *Vitya*: Diminutive of Viktor.

p. 21, *Chronicle of Current Events*: A samizdat periodical that ran from April 1968 to August 1983. A note in *Red Square at Noon* (see note to p. 7) says: "A typescript publication, circulating unofficially, though not so far illegally, in the Soviet Union and dedicated to the defence of Human Rights. It has appeared at fairly regular two-monthly intervals since April 1968 to record infringements of legality in the USSR and report at greater length on major developments in this connection." Most of the issues of the *Chronicle* were translated into English and published in the UK between 1972 and 1984.

p. 22, *"The cost of a thing... exchanged for it"*: From the first chapter ('Economy') of *Walden*, a book by the American Transcendentalist writer Henry David Thoreau (1817–62).

THE EYEWITNESS REPORT

p. 22, *Letters to a Foreign Journalist*: Changed from "*Letters to a Journalist*" for consistency with later occurrences of the title.

p. 23, *Peredelkino*: A dacha complex about fifteen miles south-west of Moscow's city centre.

p. 24, *"The heart has its reasons, which reason knows nothing about"*: From *Pensées* ("Thoughts", XXIV, 5), by the French mathematician and philosopher Blaise Pascal (1623–62).

p. 25, *a Chekhov or a Tolstoy*: The Russian writers Anton Chekhov (1860–1904) and Leo Tolstoy (1828–1910).

p. 25, *Jack London*: The American novelist, journalist and activist John Griffith Chaney (1876–1916), better known under his pseudonym Jack London.

p. 27, *In the year 1965... under pseudonyms in the West*: The two writers are Yuli Daniel (see second note to p. 13) and Andrei Sinyavsky (1925–97).

p. 27, *Khrushchev*: Nikita Khrushchev (1894–1971), First Secretary of the Communist Party of the Soviet Union from 1953 to 1964.

p. 27, *Solzhenitsyn*: The Russian author and dissident Alexander Solzhenitsyn (1918–2008), winner of the 1970 Nobel Prize in Literature.

p. 31, *the "man of steel"*: Stalin was born Joseph Vissarionovich Dzhugashvili. His adopted name is from the Russian word for "steel".

p. 36, *"Frau... Komm"*: "Lady... Come" (German).

p. 38, *7th November*: October Revolution Day, a holiday observed in Russia between 1927 and 1990.

p. 42, *Lieutenant Kijé*: A five-movement suite by Sergei Prokofiev (1891–1953).

p. 49, *the Borodin*: The Borodin Quartet, a string quartet founded in 1945 in the Soviet Union, named after the Russian composer Alexander Borodin (1833–87).

p. 49, *Beethoven*: The German composer Ludwig van Beethoven (1770–1827).

p. 50, *Obraztsov's puppet theatre*: The theatre run by the famous Russian puppeteer Sergei Obraztsov (1901–92). He toured the United States in 1963.

p. 50, *that delicious satire on Hollywood*: Possibly a reference to Obraztsov's most famous parody show, *An Unusual Concert* (1946), which satirizes bad performers.

p. 52, *Sibelius*: The Finnish composer Jean Sibelius (1865–1957).

p. 52, *Batumi*: The second-largest city in Georgia, a republic of the Soviet Union at the time in which the novel is set.

p. 52, *Tiflis*: The old name for Tbilisi, the capital of Georgia.

p. 53, *Brezhnev*: The Russian statesman Leonid Brezhnev (1906–82), General Secretary of the Communist Party of the Soviet Union from 1964 to 1982.

p. 60, *as well as nations*: The following sentence has been cut: "If that KGB Snub-Nose was as beautiful as Cleopatra and was with me right now, naked, I could no more get an erection for her than I could eat cockroaches."

p. 60, *Breslau*: The German name of the city of Wrocław in south-western Poland. The Battle of Breslau (13th February to 6th May 1945) was a three-month-long siege of the city (then held by the Germans) by the Soviet forces.

p. 61, *The International Brigades*: Military units consisting of foreign volunteers from some fifty countries that were established by the Communist International – a Soviet-backed association of national Communist parties founded in 1919, also known as the "Third International" and the "Comintern" – to assist the Popular Front government in Spain during the Spanish Civil War (1936–39).

p. 61, *Novy Mir*: A Russian literary monthly magazine founded in 1925.

p. 66, *the Ho Chi Minh trail*: A logistical network of roads and trails, named by the US after the North Vietnamese leader Ho Chi Minh, that provided manpower and materiel to the Viet Cong.

p. 67, *In vino veritas*: "In wine, there is truth" (Latin) – that is, wine makes you speak the truth.

p. 70, *Frans Hals*: The Dutch painter Frans Hals (*c*.1582–1666).

p. 74, *Sakharov, Grigorenko and Chalidze*: The Russian dissidents Andrei Sakharov (1921–89), a physicist, Petro Grigorenko (1907–87), a Soviet Army commander, and Valery Chalidze (1938–2018), a human-rights activist. Sakharov and Chalidze, together with the dissident Andrei Tverdokhlebov (1940–2011), founded the Moscow Human Rights Committee.

p. 74, *I can't stand it any more*: The preceding sentence has been cut: "I've been sitting on the fence so long I have a pole up my arse."

p. 75, *Karl Marx... "the Kingdom of Freedom"*: The German philosopher and political theorist Karl Marx (1818–83) wrote in his seminal work *Das Kapital: Kritik der politischen Ökonomie* ("Capital: A Critique of Political Economy"): "The kingdom of freedom actually begins only where labour which is determined by necessity and mundane considerations ceases" (Vol. 3, Chapter 4).

p. 78, *Article 190... social system*: As reported in a note in *Red Square at Noon* (see note to p. 7), Article 190/1 says: "The systematic dissemination by word of mouth of deliberately false fabrications slandering the Soviet state and social system, as also the preparation or dissemination of such slanderous works in written, printed or any other form, is punishable by three years' deprivation of freedom, or one year of corrective labour, or a fine of up to 100 roubles."

p. 81, *First Circle*: Solzhenitsyn was not able to get his novel *In the First Circle* published in the USSR, and the book circulated only in manuscript form. A shorter version of this work, comprising eighty-seven (rather than ninety-six) chapters and entitled *The First Circle*, was published in the UK in 1968. An English translation of the full novel was published only in 2009.

p. 82, *Sakharov's Progress... Freedom*: An essay by Andrei Sakharov (see first note to p. 74) completed in May 1968.

p. 82, *The Soviet Union: The Fifty Years*: Published in 1967 by Harcourt, Brace & World (ed. Harrison E. Salisbury), with twenty-one essays by various *New York Times* reporters.

p. 83, *Picasso*: The Spanish painter Pablo Picasso (1881–1973).

p. 84, *Konstantin Simonov*: The Soviet writer Konstantin Simonov (1915–79). *The Living and the Dead* (1959), his most famous work, is the first novel in a trilogy, which also comprises *Nobody Is Born a Soldier* (1962) and *The Last Summer* (1971). *The Living and the Dead* was published in an English translation in 1962.

p. 93, *Yesenin-Volpin*: The Russian poet and mathematician Alexander Yesenin-Volpin (1924–2016), a prominent dissident figure who was interned in a psychiatric hospital in 1968. He emigrated to the USA in May 1972.

p. 93, *Samsonov*: The geophysicist Nikolai Samsonov (1906–72), the recipient of a Stalin Prize for his Arctic research, "was interned in the Leningrad psychiatric hospital from 1956 to 1964, after writing to the Central Committee of the CPSU criticizing some of Stalin's theoretical propositions" (*Nature*, Vol. 226, 20th June 1970, p. 1080).

p. 108, *the Patriotic War*: A term used in Russia to describe the struggle against Nazi Germany following the latter's attempted invasion of the Soviet Union beginning in June 1941.

p. 112, *Gorky, Hugo, Balzac*: The Russian writer Maxim Gorky (1868–1936), the French poet and novelist Victor Hugo (1802–85) and the French novelist Honoré de Balzac (1799–1850).

p. 112, *And Quiet Flows the Don*: A novel written between 1925 and 1940 by the Russian author Mikhail Sholokhov (1905–84), winner of the Nobel Prize in Literature in 1965. Sholokhov's authorship of the book has been widely disputed.

p. 116, *the Literary Gazette*: *Literaturnaya Gazeta*, a cultural and political periodical founded in 1830, which was published until 1831, reappeared in the period 1840–49 and was revived in 1929.

p. 117, *In one of his letters... I forget*: The Chekhov quotation cannot be traced, and may be fictitious.

p. 117, *Serbsky Institute of Forensic Psychiatry*: Founded in 1921, and now called Serbsky Centre.

p. 120, *Babi Yar*: The site (in modern Ukraine) of a famous massacre committed by the Nazis against the Jews on 29th–30th September 1941. Further massacres of Jews and other ethnic groups were carried out on the same site on later dates.

p. 121, *Andrei D. Sakharov*: See first note to p. 74. Sakharov's patronymic was Dmitrievich.

p. 125, *Pyotr Yakir*: The Russian historian and dissident Pyotr Yakir (1923–82).

p. 125, *paving his way back*: Amended from "paying his way back" in the original typescript.

p. 138, *Karl Marx... "Struggle"*: The anecdote may be fictitious, but in *Das Kapital* (see note to p. 75), Vol. 1, Chapter 25, Section 5a, Marx quoted from William Ewart Gladstone's (1809–98) speech in the House of Commons on 7th April 1864: "What is human life but, in the majority of cases, a struggle for existence?"

p. 140, *a passage in one of Lenin's works... officials*: It is possible that this concept was also expressed or quoted by Lenin, but the source here appears to be Andrei Sakharov, who in *Progress, Coexistence and Intellectual Freedom* (see first note to p. 82) says: "Marx once wrote that the illusion that the 'bosses know everything best' and 'only the higher circles familiar with the official nature of things can pass judgement' was held by officials who equate the public weal with government authority" (Chapter 7, 'The Threat to Intellectual Freedom'). Marx's original citation could not be traced.

NOTES

p. 141, *Sulfazin*: Sulfozinum, a pharmaceutical drug that causes high body temperature and severe pain. In the Soviet Union, it was used in the treatment of syphilitic encephalitis, various psychiatric conditions and alcoholism.

p. 142, *Just because... for even longer*: From 'Advice to a Fellow Prisoner', a poem by the Turkish poet Nâzım Hikmet (1902–63).

p. 143, *Not long before President Kennedy... "Life is not fair"*: The US President John F. Kennedy (1917–63) was assassinated on 22nd November 1963. Although his actual words, during a speech on TV, were "Who said life is fair?", they were widely reported by the press as "Life is not fair".

p. 144, *Kuybyshev*: Now the city of Samara, about 1,000 km south-east of Moscow.

p. 145, *secret report that Khrushchev... Communist Party*: Khrushchev delivered his famous "secret report" speech on 25th February 1956.

p. 148, *Murmansk*: A city and port on the Barents Sea, about 1,850 km north of Moscow and 200 km north of the Arctic Circle.

p. 150, *Stelazine*: An antipsychotic drug normally used to treat schizophrenia.

p. 151, *Galich*: The Soviet singer-songwriter and dissident Alexander Ginzburg, better known under his pseudonym Alexander Galich (1918–77). Galich was expelled from the Moscow branch of the Writers' Union on 29th December 1971. The verses quoted immediately afterwards are from one of his best-known songs, 'The Prospectors' Little Waltz'.

p. 154, *haloperidol*: Another antipsychotic normally used to treat schizophrenia.

p. 163, *the Writers' Union... moved to expel Solzhenitsyn*: Solzhenitsyn was expelled from the Writers' Union in 1969.

CALDER PUBLICATIONS
EDGY TITLES FROM A LEGENDARY LIST

www.calderpublications.com